Brandi's car dangled precariously over the deep ravine. Through the uncanny silence, a child's scream sent chills down his neck.

A child? He hurried toward the car and called out, "Brandi, don't move." His boots slid in the mud as he stepped off the road toward the wreckage.

"Rhett..." Her voice was shrill. "Help us!"

"Are you hurt?"

"No, I don't think so. The car's going to fall. Get us out of here!"

"Hold on. You'll be fine. Just don't move."

Behind his back seat, he had a small toolbox. The tie strap inside was only fifteen feet long. He hoped it was enough to reach her back bumper.

"Brandi, just a few more seconds and I'll have you out of there."

Brandi thought he'd let her down before, but this time he wouldn't. No matter their past, he'd do everything in his power to keep her safe.

A cracking sound had him turning as a branch splintered.

Strap in hand, he moved toward the back of the car, praying he could secure the vehicle before the car plummeted, taking all three of them with it.

Until recently, **Connie Queen** has spent all of her life in Texas, where she met and married her high school sweetheart. Together they've raised eight children and are enjoying their grandchildren. Today she resides with her husband and Nash, her Great Dane, in Nebraska, where she's working on her next heart-throbbing suspense.

Books by Connie Queen

Love Inspired Suspense

Justice Undercover
Texas Christmas Revenge

Visit the Author Profile page at Harlequin.com.

TEXAS
CHRISTMAS
REVENGE

CONNIE QUEEN

LOVE INSPIRED SUSPENSE
INSPIRATIONAL ROMANCE

LOVE INSPIRED® SUSPENSE
INSPIRATIONAL ROMANCE

Recycling programs for this product may not exist in your area.

ISBN-13: 978-1-335-55466-6

Texas Christmas Revenge

Copyright © 2021 by Connie Queen

This edition published by arrangement with Harlequin Books S.A.

For questions and comments about the quality of this book, please contact us at CustomerService@Harlequin.com.

Love Inspired
22 Adelaide St. West, 40th Floor
Toronto, Ontario M5H 4E3, Canada
www.Harlequin.com

Printed in U.S.A.

Trust in the Lord with all thine heart;
and lean not unto thine own understanding.
—*Proverbs* 3:5

This book is dedicated to my mom, Lillie Lou Monk,
a sweet Christian lady who always wore a smile,
could cook a meal for a crowd at a moment's notice,
and never said no to going and doing things.
As a kid, I remember her reading books and, later,
working at a library. Even though she never got to see
my dream of becoming an author come true,
she would've really gotten a kick out of it and
would've wanted to celebrate. Thanks for being you.

I'd like to acknowledge Shannon Haines,
a friend who has more than once answered my questions
about emergency dispatchers.

As always, thank you to my wonderful critique partners:
Rhonda, Sharee, Jackie and Sherrinda.
You ladies are the best.

ONE

*C*lunk.

Brandi Callahan spun around, her eyes landing on the tack room. The muffled sound made it impossible to make out the source.

Cold seeped into her very being, making her regret leaving her coat on the back of her office chair. She'd sprinted out of the emergency dispatch office so fast she hadn't been thinking after that call from her sister.

Her *presumed-dead* sister.

She shivered as she waited at the door of her grandparents' barn, miles from nowhere at four thirty in the morning, wondering if she should have waited until daybreak to come. But how could she not come if Sadie were truly alive? A quick check of her grandparents' vacant three-story Victorian house had turned up nothing but scurrying rodents and a deep yearning for family—a reminder of all Brandi had lost.

"Sadie," she called.

It took a moment for Brandi's eyes to adjust, as a beam of light shone through the cracks of the barn door from her headlights onto old square bales of hay. A tiny blind spot in her left eye made it easy to miss details, so she adjusted her view to make certain she didn't miss anything. A noise sounded somewhere in the distance. More rodents? She glanced over her shoulder, the headlights blinding her. Hairs stood up on the back of her neck. "Sadie, are you here?"

As soon as she moved deeper into the old structure, darkness overtook her.

Ding. This time, there was no mistaking something had moved. It wasn't only the creaks of an ancient building.

"Sadie." She said the name a little louder. If anyone was nearby, they would've already heard her movement and seen her Cavalier outside, so there wasn't any reason to be quiet. Even louder, she called, "Sadie. Please come out."

This time when the scuffling resonated, her gaze fell on Grandpa's truck. When they were kids, she and Sadie used to play in the seat and pretend to drive. She crossed the room and yanked open the rusty truck door.

Two frightened eyes stared back at her. A dark-haired little boy, no more than eighteen months old, huddled with his blanket and a stuffed Christmas-reindeer teddy bear. His lips trembled with fear.

Brandi's heart took a nosedive. Who would leave a toddler alone on a farm, miles from any other homes in the cold? Someone desperate, that's who. Did her sister leave this precious boy? The thought stunned her. "It's okay, little fellow. Here, let's get you warm."

"No," he cried and crawled to the other side of the cab. The denim blanket flipped over, and she read the name Levi embroidered in red in the corner.

"Levi…"

He looked up. She didn't blame him for being scared;

she kept her voice low and soothing. "Is that your name? Levi? My name is Brandi. I won't hurt you."

His lip puckered and his eyebrows turned down, giving her a don't-touch-me warning.

"Are you hungry? I have a doughnut in my car." A half-eaten doughnut.

Before the boy could answer, an engine revved from outside. Gravel sprayed as a vehicle came to a stop.

Panic driving her, and not understanding what was going on, she reached across the seat and grabbed the boy along with the bear and his blanket. Getting to her vehicle wasn't an option. She dashed for the barn's side exit. Before she made it, the main door swung open and a burly, bearded man with a gun stepped inside.

"Stop!"

She didn't obey but slammed into the small side door, knocking it wide. Clinging to the boy, she raced for the house.

Almost every day for the last few years she'd dealt with a wide range of crises as an emergency dispatcher, but she had sat safely behind a desk. She didn't like being on this side of danger.

A shot rang out.

Her heart stampeded in her chest. What was going on? What had Sadie gotten herself into? She could barely see as she took the porch steps two at a time to the side door of her grandparents' home and then slung the screen door open. With hands shaking, she hurried inside and slammed it so hard the knob didn't latch. The little fella whimpered as she started to dash upstairs. But no, that was where the bearded man would expect her to hide. Instead, she ran past the wooden dining table and into the small pantry in the corner of the kitchen. She knocked a pile of brown paper sacks and an old ice cream maker out of the way.

Just as she slid to the floor with her back against the wall, footsteps pounded across the wooden porch. The kitchen door screeched open, causing her lungs to freeze. She leaned to the side, hoping the mop and broom would cover her. But that was silly. If nothing else, she could use the broomstick as a weapon.

Levi's brown eyes connected with hers as boots scuffled across the linoleum floor in the kitchen. As if the toddler sensed the danger, he remained silent, and she pulled him against her chest and softly whispered against his ear, "It's okay."

Movement outside the pantry stopped, and she pictured the man listening. She didn't breathe. *Please don't let him sense we're in here.* Silent seconds ticked by.

Finally, footsteps headed across the wooden floor to the stairs. As soon as the man was on the second floor, she repositioned her grip on the boy, climbed to her feet and tiptoed fast out the door. She closed the door and sprinted for her car. A commotion sounded from the house, but she ran for her life, not turning to look.

"Stop! Jarvis County Sheriff's Department. Brandi Callahan, let me see your hands."

What? The unexpected but familiar male voice shocked her, causing her to stutter-step. A Jarvis County sheriff's deputy stood with his gun raised. She wasn't doing anything wrong. Brandi stumbled while yelling, "There's a man with a gun in the house. He shot at me."

"Stop."

"I can't… Please."

Just then, a shot rang out from the porch. Confusion and anger etched across the officer's face as he did a double take at the gunman. "Get to cover, Callahan," Deputy Norris barked as he moved behind the back of his car.

Brandi ran and then slid inside her own car as the deputy talked into his mic.

"I need backup now, at the Callahan farm."

Suddenly, more popping broke the silence.

Pings bounced off the deputy's hood, and the windshield shattered.

Levi screamed as Brandi turned the key in the ignition.

Deputy Norris fell to the ground.

A shriek escaped her throat. Disbelief shook her. Without a moment's thought, she threw her car into gear. The boy clung to her neck, making it difficult to see as she flew down the drive. She couldn't tell if the gunman followed her, but she had to assume he would.

Her hands shook as frightened tears rolled down her cheeks. Nervous for the boy's safety, she hit the brakes and placed him in the passenger seat and put the seat belt on him.

Who was this guy? Where was Sadie?

Two years ago, everything Brandi had ever believed in—family, love and security—had been ripped away in a matter of weeks, engulfing her life in bitterness and resentment. Her father was accused of stealing, and then apparently killed himself. This was followed by Sadie's disappearance, making Brandi question if her sister had something to do with the theft. Authorities believed Sadie was dead, but Brandi didn't buy it.

If it was the last thing Brandi did, she aimed to prove her father's innocence and restore the family's reputation. And she planned to start by finding her sister.

If she lived that long.

A glance over her shoulder showed headlights on the treetops of her grandparents' drive. He was coming for her. She floored it. All she could think was that she had to get away.

Faster.

Faster.

Texas Ranger Rhett Kincaid ran his fingers through his damp hair as he stepped into his kitchen. He didn't have to be at work until seven this morning, so he'd taken advantage and gotten in a couple of quick miles on the treadmill before he took a shower and dressed. He grabbed a K-cup from his cabinet, planning to make coffee, when headlights shot through the kitchen window. He glanced out and saw a car speeding down his driveway. Who would be here at five fifteen in the morning?

He retrieved his gun from the top of the refrigerator, stepped into his boots and strode to the front door, prepared for trouble. As he looked out, the headlights went off and the silhouette of a woman scrambled out of a coupe. His eyes narrowed as he tried to make out her identity, but a light fog hung in the air. Rhett's house sat at the edge of town, the last property on a dead-end road. Not necessarily in the boonies, but no one drove out this way unless they were visiting him or were lost.

He stepped out on the porch. "Can I help you?"

She looked up, her shoulder-length blond hair blew across her face, and their eyes collided. His throat tightened as realization hit him that the woman was Brandi Callahan. It had been two years since he'd laid eyes on her.

Momentarily caught off guard, he hesitated before he crossed the wooden porch. Just then a jacked-up vehicle whipped into the drive and barreled toward Brandi's coupe.

She jumped back into her car.

"Wait!" He hurried down the steps.

Gunfire ripped through the night. A bullet whizzed past his ear.

Brandi hit the gas, mud flying as she peeled out of the drive, the SUV right on her tail. Rhett ran for his truck.

Possible scenarios ran through his mind, but he couldn't fathom why someone was after Brandi. He took off in the direction of the two vehicles. One thing was clear: if she had been looking to *him* for help, that meant she was in deep trouble. Brandi wanted nothing to do with him.

Rhett was familiar with the back roads, and though he took them at high speed, he couldn't see taillights in front of him. Hazardous curves littered the road.

He accelerated even more, and after a couple of minutes, the red glow of taillights came into view. Thankfully, the half-frozen ground prohibited dust clouds. He closed the distance on the SUV. Brandi's taillights were just ahead. He had to do something, but sixty-five miles per hour was much too fast to shoot at her pursuer. He moved in and identified the vehicle as an older brown-and-white Ford Bronco.

As they entered a long straightaway, Rhett's truck hit a deep pothole and jolted. He barely kept it under control. He needed to get this guy off the road and planned to perform a PIT maneuver. The Bronco sped up. Rhett gripped the steering wheel tight at the upcoming curve in the road.

Please, Brandi, slow down. Even though she had broken off their engagement, Rhett hadn't stopped thinking about her. He hated the way things had ended between them and had never understood how she could dump him so easily after agreeing to marry. After his father had abandoned their family, Rhett had put commitment with a capital *C* at the top of his own list of priorities. Evidently, Brandi didn't feel the same way.

But no matter what Rhett said or how he tried to help with the disappearance of her sister, Brandi had lumped him together with the Mulberry Gap citizens who she felt had turned their back on her during her time of need.

Desperate to get the man off her bumper, Rhett closed in and clipped the Bronco's rear. The SUV fishtailed, red taillights dancing in the mist, and then slid through the curve on two wheels. The Bronco hit the ground again and regained control. The driver slammed on his brakes. Rhett had expected the move and dodged the back end, pulling to the right of the Bronco. Rhett slowed down until he was again behind the vehicle.

A mile or so ahead was a sharp T. Did Brandi remember it was ahead?

He had to end this now. Again, he floored his truck and with his heavy-duty grill guard, clipped the left side of the Bronco's bumper, sending it sideways and out of control. The monster vehicle bounced and slammed into the ditch. Rhett hit his brakes, expecting the Bronco to get stuck in the trench, but the engine roared, the large tires sending mud flying.

Rhett grabbed his gun and exited his vehicle. He watched as the Bronco gained traction, plowed through a barbwire fence and fled through a pasture. He didn't wait but jumped back in his truck and took off to find Brandi.

His heart pounded, praying she was all right. He didn't know why this guy had chased his ex-fiancée, but his intent had been deadly. Rhett grabbed his phone and tried to call Brandi's phone, hoping her number hadn't changed. The call went straight to voice mail.

As he approached the T in the road, he slowed, his headlight beams bouncing from the treetops. His gaze latched onto skid marks—the lines went from the middle of the road and disappeared straight ahead. An eerie glow illuminated the deep ravine. Fog filtered through the air.

He came to a stop and jogged to the edge of the rock road.

His breath hitched as he eyed the back of her car. Taillights glowed in the steam that lifted from the hood. Her car dangled precariously over the deep ravine. The small, bare tree branches bent, ready to snap any second as the front end slightly bounced up and down.

Through the uncanny silence, a child's scream sent chills down his neck.

A child? He hurried toward the car and called out, "Brandi, don't move." His boots slid in the mud as he stepped off the road toward the wreckage. "Are you hurt?"

"Rhett…" Her voice was shrill. "Help us!"

"Are you hurt?" he repeated.

"No, I don't think so. The car's going to fall. Get us out of here!"

"Hold on." The fear in her voice ramped up his already elevated adrenaline. "You'll be fine. Just don't move."

A rope or chain. His mind whirled, trying to remember what he had in his truck. Behind his back seat he had a small toolbox. He opened it, and his heart swelled. An unopened tie strap, just like he thought. It was only fifteen feet long, but it was all he had. He hoped it was enough to reach her back bumper. He jumped in the truck and pulled close to the edge of the ravine. Still too far away. He eased forward a little more until the truck's front end nosedived alarmingly near the rim.

He got out and hurried to his front bumper to secure the strap. "I've almost got it, Brandi. Just a few more seconds and I'll have you out of there."

Brandi thought he'd let her down before, but this time he wouldn't. No matter their past, and even if their breakup had hurt more than he let anyone know, he'd do everything in his power to keep her safe. She'd made the right decision running to him.

A cracking sound had him turning as a branch splintered. And then several more snapped as Brandi's car dropped downward.

"Rhett!"

His heart constricted.

Strap in hand, he moved for the back of the car, praying he could secure the vehicle before the car plummeted, taking all three of them with it.

TWO

"Rhett!" Brandi yelled again and leaned back in the seat as far as she could. Her feet dug into the floorboard as she stood straight up, trying not to send the unbalanced coupe into the ravine below.

Levi bawled in the passenger seat while yelling, "Mommy!"

She turned to the little guy. He must be scared to death—his world had turned upside down. "It's all right, Levi. Hold tight."

The car jerked again. Brandi tried to keep her voice down so as to not frighten the boy. "We're falling."

"Hold on," Rhett hollered from the ditch beside her. "Roll down your window and try not to move."

Her Cavalier swayed on the flimsy branches and her hand trembled as she hit the electric window button. It whizzed down.

"I'll throw the end of the strap to you. Tie it around yourself."

"What about the baby? I need to get him out." Brandi squeezed her eyes shut and prayed. *Please, don't let us fall*.

"Okay. Let me try something else."

Her heart raced, and a shadow crossed the headlights streaming through her back window, followed by the roar of his truck. Two years wasn't a long time not to see a person, unless he had been your best friend. Right now, it seemed like an eternity since Rhett had been a part of her life. Relief he had chased after her flowed through her very being. Of course, considering his protective nature, she had known he would. A truck door slammed and then a clicking on her bumper. She didn't breathe.

Don't fall. Don't fall. She kept repeating the prayer.

Her car shook. She was tempted to turn around to see what he was doing, but she didn't dare.

The swishing of footsteps in the dead grass drew her attention.

"The strap is hooked to your bumper. It should be secure."

Should be? That didn't make her feel better.

Rhett came up to her window. The ditch was so steep the car was slightly above him. "Can you get the baby?"

"I don't know. I'm afraid movement will make the car fall."

"I'll hold the car steady as much as I can." His hand clutched the door through the window opening.

"No, don't do that. If the strap breaks the car might hit you." As desperate as the situation was, she couldn't bear it if Rhett was injured because of her.

"Brandi, it's the only way. We don't have much time. Get the baby."

"Okay." She leaned over the passenger seat and the car tilted to the right. She froze.

"I've got it. Keep going."

The ravine was deep enough that if the car fell, it could easily roll forward or land on its top. Normally, many of the creeks and ravines were dry, but they'd received rain lately. She grabbed Levi's arm as he continued to cry, and then released the seat belt latch. In one swift move, she swung the child, along with his blanket, against her chest, expecting the car to plummet. "I've got him."

"When I open the door, jump into my arms."

The car dipped even more to the right, the front-end nose-diving toward the dark ravine. "We'll fall."

"Trust me, Brandi. We have no choice. Move now."

Trust him. She took a deep breath. Just as the car lurched forward a couple more feet, they fell into Rhett's arms.

The impact dropped him to one knee on the steep incline. The car swung to the right and then back toward them. He yelled, "Out of the way."

He tackled her to the frosty ground, Levi protectively tucked under her arm. Rhett's muscular body pressed into her back, shielding them as the car whizzed past, the movement creating a blast of air, and then shifted the other way. "Go. Get up the bank."

All three of them scrambled up the incline and made it to solid ground as another limb broke. The coupe dangled back and forth when the strap snapped.

The car plunged into the lower trees, hit on its front bumper, slowly pitched forward and landed upside down in the water.

He spun around. "Would you like to tell me what's going on?"

Brandi moved farther away from the edge of the ravine. Her heart continued to pound as the fear of what could've been hit home. She shivered. "I need help."

"I can see that." Rhett's gaze connected with hers,

concern carved in his expression. "You're freezing. Let's
get in my truck and you can explain."

She hurried around to the passenger side while he
untied the harness from his front bumper. He tossed
the broken piece in the bed of his truck, climbed inside
and moved the truck away from the bank. His Wran-
gler Retro jeans, untucked white button-down shirt and
leather boots indicated he was probably dressing for
work when she arrived this morning. The razor stubble
along his chiseled chin said she'd interrupted his morning routine. Rhett Kincaid had grown even more handsome since she'd last seen him. Who would've thought
that was possible?

He turned dark, chocolate-colored eyes on her. "Let's
have it. What was that all about?"

Rhett had always been the protective type, which was
why he was a good lawman. *Except when it came to finding Sadie*, she thought bitterly. Brandi didn't like to ask
for help. Actually, she despised seeking any assistance
after her friends and the town had turned their backs on
her two years ago by accusing her family of stealing a
fund set up for the residents. She'd grown up in Mulberry
Gap, Texas. Her father had a stellar reputation in the community, but yet, when money went missing from the fund
he'd been in charge of, the citizens—and even the sheriff's department—were quick to point the finger at him.

Even Rhett had joined the ranks of the traitors when
she needed him most, by dropping Sadie's disappearance case after only six months. Did she have a choice
but to tell Rhett that her sister had called 911? Would he
believe Sadie was alive?

Probably not.

Brandi didn't want to chance an argument. "Since my

car is ruined, do you think you can give me a ride to my mom's house?"

He sighed. "Come on, Callahan. This is more serious than that. That guy in the Bronco nearly killed you. Who was he, and whose kid is that?"

As if sensing he was the topic of the conversation, Levi whined and laid his head on her chest. "It's a long story. The *kid* is Levi. I don't know my attacker or why he came after me. I just need to borrow a car."

Rhett frowned. "Listen, we didn't part on good terms, but I don't want to see you hurt. Why don't you come back to my house and have a cup of coffee while you fill me in?"

"I can't do that." She wasn't certain, but she thought the bearded man had shot Deputy Norris. If so, then the sheriff's department could be looking for her. She needed a place to recoup while she figured out what was going on. The Jarvis County Sheriff's Department and the Callahans didn't exactly get along. "I appreciate your offer, but I've got this."

He scrutinized her. "There's something you're not telling me. I know that you and a few of the citizens of Mulberry Gap don't see eye to eye."

"That's a nice way of putting it," she snorted. "They believe my family is guilty of stealing over a million dollars, and it's not just the citizens, but the sheriff's department, as well."

"Brandi, that's not true. The sheriff's department was just doing their job. Your father oversaw the disaster fund and after his death, Sadie—"

"Stop. I'm not going to discuss my family." She held up her hand. To this day, she couldn't talk about the accusation against her father without her stomach twisting into painful knots. The fund he'd been charged with embezzling had been set up for victims of the double tornadoes that tore through the town of Mulberry Gap.

Over the last two years, she'd worked hard and prayed often to rein in her emotions along with the deep bitterness she harbored against the townspeople. No matter how suspicious the circumstances, her daddy was not a thief. The man who'd sat through endless school sporting events, read Bible stories and tucked her in every night had been the epitome of integrity.

Then why did he kill himself? Guilty conscience? Angrily, she shoved the question to the back of her mind.

Many of Mulberry Gap's residents had lost their homes, some who had too little or no home insurance. While her heart went out to those who suffered, she knew that just because her father oversaw the fund at the bank didn't mean he took the money.

Rhett stared at her with an expression she couldn't read. If she didn't know better, she would've thought it was hurt in his eyes. Finally, he sighed. "You can trust *me.*"

She trusted no one.

Rhett put his truck into gear and turned around in the road, frustration eating at him. Didn't Brandi understand he was on her side? Even though she had made it clear she wasn't interested in a romantic relationship, she ought to understand that he cared for her safety. He stole a quick glance at her. Despite her messed-up hair and her obvious state of distress, she looked good in her comfy blue long-sleeved T-shirt, jeans and running shoes. The blue brought out the sapphire in her eyes—even the hazy dot on her left iris from her injury was barely detectable. It was disconcerting that just being close to her could have this kind of effect on him.

As he headed back in the other direction, a vehicle with flashing lights came speeding toward them. A sheriff's vehicle. "Did you call the sheriff's department?"

"No, of course not. There was no time." Her voice held a tinge of concern. "Please, if that *is* the sheriff's department, don't let them take me in."

The vehicle stopped in front of them, the lights still swirling.

Why did she fear they had come for her? He stared at her. "Brandi, what's going on? I'm a Texas Ranger, the sheriff's my uncle. If you're guilty of—"

"I'm not guilty. You know me better than that." A funny expression crossed her face. "Look, I'll tell you everything once the deputy leaves, I promise. Just please don't let him arrest me."

The quiver in her voice shouted panic. What had she gotten herself into? Rhett rolled down his window as the deputy approached. It was Deputy Dan Coble. He was an older officer and a good man, but he'd lost his barn in the tornado and had been one of the townspeople who'd been upset at the missing money.

"Can I help you, Deputy?"

Coble shined a flashlight at Rhett, temporarily blinding him and then across the seat at Brandi. She glanced away until he pointed the instrument at the back seat. Then the deputy looked over his shoulder to the ravine. Rhett didn't know if he could see her car, but surely the tracks were noticeable. "I need to search your truck."

"What is the reason? We have the right to be informed of the cause."

"We have a deputy down over at the Callahan farm.

Shot. We have reason to believe Brandi may've been the shooter."

"I did not." She leaned across the seat, and Rhett reached over and squeezed her hand.

Coble looked at Rhett. "When the deputy called in, he said the only person on the premises was Brandi Callahan."

Brandi whispered, so only he could hear, "That's not true."

Rhett kept his expression even and his gaze on the deputy. A downed officer? Every law officer in the county would be trying to solve the case, and he prayed Brandi wasn't the prime suspect. "Sir, you realize I have a weapon in my vehicle."

"Uh, yes, I of course know that, Rhett. But I still need to look." Coble rubbed the back of his neck nervously, like he didn't want to question Rhett. For two good reasons. Rhett was a Texas Ranger, and he was the sheriff's nephew. "I need you all to step out of the vehicle."

Rhett could deny him the right to search, but he knew there was nothing incriminating in his vehicle. It would be best to cooperate, at this point. He glanced her way. "It's cold out here, but the search shouldn't take long."

"I understand." She regarded the baby. The little fellow snuggled even closer as she climbed out and wrapped his blanket around him.

Rhett retrieved his Stetson from the back seat and shoved it on his head, and then he grabbed his fleece-lined Carhartt jacket and put it over her shoulders. The coat swallowed her, but it had never stopped her from wearing his things when they were dating. There was something satisfying about seeing Brandi in his jacket. He turned his attention back to Coble. "I have a weapon in the console and another in my backpack in the back seat."

The older man nodded and preceded to go through the truck.

"I wasn't the only person at the farm," Brandi whispered. "That guy in the Bronco shot at me."

Rhett held up his hand indicating they'd discuss it later.

Coble turned off his flashlight and stepped back from the vehicle. Rhett was relieved he didn't take long.

What was Brandi hiding? What would Coble have done if she'd been alone? Take her in?

The deputy gave her a slight smile. "Get that little boy back in the warmth of the truck."

Rhett waited while she climbed in, before he did the same.

Coble asked her, "Who does that boy belong to? You don't have a child, do you, Miss Callahan?"

Rhett glanced at her, too. She hadn't answered when he'd asked.

"I'm taking care of him for a friend."

"Which friend?" Coble aimed the question at her.

Brandi's eyes narrowed. "Someone who no longer lives around here."

"Okay. Looks like your car went into the ditch." The deputy frowned, like he didn't want to say the next words. "I need you to come to the department for questioning."

Before she could answer, Rhett jumped in. "Deputy Coble, someone attacked Brandi. He was driving a Ford Bronco. I didn't get his license plate, but I saw him. Tried to catch him, but he got away from me in Bill Reeny's pasture. I'm sure if you wait until daylight, we can find the tracks. I'll call my uncle and inform him of the situation. I'm grateful for your help."

Coble chewed on his lip, like he was uncertain what to do. Or was that anger he attempted to hide? Coble wouldn't be the first deputy to show resentment toward Rhett for the family connection to the sheriff. Finally, Coble asked, "Did you get a good look at the man in the Bronco?"

"No."

The deputy nodded. "Fine. I'll need Brandi's number if we need to get ahold of her."

"I appreciate that." Rhett gave the deputy the information.

The deputy glanced back toward the ravine. "It's possible we'll need to check out her car, too. But if we do, we'll let you know. Have a good day."

"Okay." Rhett rolled up the window as he pulled away, leaving the deputy in the road.

"Thanks."

He drew in a breath. "Brandi, he never would've let you go if Uncle Duke wasn't the sheriff. I don't like using my relationship to pull strings like that. Tell me what happened. Someone shot a deputy. This is serious."

"I didn't shoot anyone. You've got to believe that." She then proceeded to give him a rundown of the events—finding the toddler in a pickup, the gunman showing up, hiding in the house and then taking off in her car after Deputy Norris was shot.

Brandi had always been truthful, sometimes to the point of being painfully honest, so he didn't doubt the fantastic story. But she was holding back. If she would just trust him… "What made you go out to your grandparents' farm in the middle of the night? How did you know a baby would be there?"

"I didn't know a baby was there." Her tone screamed defensive.

"Spit it out."

A deep frown created tiny lines across her forehead. "Listen. I appreciate your help, but I only need a ride to Mom's so I can get a car. I won't bother you again."

He coolly propped his hand across the steering wheel and pulled over to the side of the road. He waited while Deputy Coble's SUV passed with the lights off, before he turned to her. "I'm worried about you. That guy intended to hurt, maybe even kill you. I can't stand by and do nothing when you're in trouble. Why won't you let me help you?"

Levi began to squirm, and she repositioned him on her shoulder. "I'll be fine."

"And this boy who belongs to a *friend*. You can protect him, too?"

Brandi nodded.

Stubborn woman. He drew a calming breath. She'd changed; her easygoing manner had hardened. After her father's death and Sadie's disappearance, Brandi seemed distrustful of everyone. She'd been severely hurt. He had witnessed her wariness with coworkers and the sheriff's department. Dispatchers spent a lot of the time on the phone communicating with first responders, and Brandi's attitude had gone from friendly to businesslike. She'd built a wall so thick and tall no one could get close. From what he'd heard, Brandi's relationship with her mother had suffered, too.

What bothered him the most was that Brandi had thrown him in the can't-be-trusted category, as well. But like it or not, he wasn't going to sit by and let her endanger herself now.

The boy whined. He might not be safe, either. The thin, long-sleeved shirt, cotton pants and socks he was wearing weren't enough to keep him warm. Rhett would buy the boy some new clothes later today.

"Can we go?" Impatience tinged her reply. "Levi's bound to be hungry."

"You promised."

"What?" She stared at him.

He'd use whatever means necessary to help her. Whatever Brandi's issues, she always kept her word. "You promised you'd tell me everything if I kept the sheriff's department from taking you in. Why did you go to your grandparents' farm in the middle of the night?"

She opened her mouth as if she were going to argue, then shut it again. She lifted her chin. "Sadie called in last night."

Surprise shook him, but he managed to rein in a response and remained cool. "At dispatch. Like an emergency call?"

"Yes." She sat even straighter, daring him to contradict her. "Before the call disconnected, the only words she got out was 'the farm.' We both know that's my grandparents' place."

He nodded and put the truck into gear, pulling onto the road.

"What? You don't believe me?" She grabbed the dash and twisted toward him. "Where are we going?"

Unbeknownst to Brandi, Rhett had previously had one of the Texas Rangers investigators look into finding her sister so that Brandi could have closure, but the effort had produced nothing except a cold trail originating the night Sadie disappeared. "We're going to the dispatch office to listen to the 911 recording. If Sadie left this boy alone, she must be in deep trouble."

Brandi blinked in surprise.

Two years ago, he'd been new to the Rangers, and couldn't involve himself in the case because his lieutenant believed his close connection to Brandi would be a conflict of interest. But his obligation to her went deeper than that this time, and he had no intention of making the same mistake as before. The second she pulled into his drive with a gunman on her tail, desperate for help, he was involved. She would not be left to fight this battle alone.

No matter the cost.

THREE

Suspicion swirled in Brandi's gut. Was this a game? "You believe Sadie's alive?"

"I'm not certain what I think about Sadie and this boy. Let's say I'm cautious. You went to your grandparents' place because you thought your sister called. It bears checking out."

Fair enough. That was more than she had expected from Rhett Kincaid, especially since their last conversation two years ago had ended in a full-blown shouting match when he tried to convince her Sadie was dead—the last painful straw that caused her to break off their engagement. She couldn't marry a man who didn't stand by her.

At this point, she wasn't sure she could have a serious relationship with any man. Except for a few people, everyone had turned against her, even those she'd known her entire life. How could she ever put her faith in someone again? She was better off leaning on herself and God alone.

She called Shannon Woolsey, her boss, and asked if they could listen to the 911 recording. Shannon agreed to have it ready.

Levi snuggled against her, and his dark eyes remained closed longer with each blink. A smile came to her lips. He was such a quiet and sweet boy. Since finding him in the truck, the realization Levi must be her nephew had finally sunk in. Sadie had a child. A deep protectiveness consumed her. She planned to do everything in her power to reunite Levi with Sadie.

Brandi had hoped to have kids one day, but when she called off the engagement, she had put that plan on the back burner. The day her dad died was the day her life had begun to career out of control. Not only did doubt cloud her memories of her perfect childhood and family, but the scandal had ripped apart her future, as well.

Rhett's cell phone rang, and he answered on the Bluetooth speaker. "Kincaid."

"Rhett, are you okay? Your uncle called and told me you'd been involved in a high-speed chase."

Brandi kept her gaze straight ahead but there was no pretending not to overhear the call from Rhett's aunt Lauren. News traveled fast. The woman had been hospitable while she and Rhett dated, offering them a standing invitation for lunch every Sunday after worship services. Even though they occasionally took her up on her offer, she and Rhett spent most Sundays with Brandi's side of the family. It was no secret that when Rhett's father abandoned his wife and kids, and when his mama gave in to alcohol, his aunt and uncle had stepped in to fill that void for him and his sister.

"I'm fine, Aunt Lauren. Law enforcement comes with risks."

"Oh, I know." She laughed. "Duke tells me all the time I worry too much, but I wouldn't be much of an aunt if

I wasn't concerned for your safety." There was a pause. "Is Brandi with you?"

Brandi leaned toward the mic. "I'm here."

"So good to hear your voice. You need to come by sometime and visit with Duke and me. Meredith and Wes would enjoy seeing you two again."

She doubted that. Meredith and Wes were Duke and Lauren's two kids. Meredith was a fashion model who was living outside of New York City and Wes, after a struggle with drug abuse, had finally got a job at the sheriff's department—no doubt due to his father's influence.

Rhett glanced at her. "Aunt Lauren, we'll have to get a rain check on the visit for now."

"I understand. I miss seeing you. Come by anytime and stay safe."

"I will." He clicked off.

Brandi might have a bad taste for the sheriff's department, but she couldn't deny Rhett's family had always been welcoming to her. "Lauren is a nice lady."

"Yes, she is. I think since her kids have moved out of the house, she has a lot of time on her hands. Family is everything to her." Rhett glanced at her and Levi. "I'll get him something to eat at the store before we get to the dispatch office."

"I'd appreciate that."

"We also need a safety seat. I'll stop at the all-night mega store and pick up one if you want to stay in the truck with him and keep the heater going."

She wouldn't mind buying Levi some things, but Rhett was right, the little guy looked exhausted; it would be better if she kept him in the vehicle so he'd continue to sleep. "Thanks."

Rhett pulled in and parked. His gaze held hers a little longer than necessary, with a softness she couldn't describe. If she didn't know better, she'd think he was taken with Levi. Ten minutes later, he returned lugging a big box, a bag of diapers and several plastic shopping bags. "Here. I didn't know what he liked, so I picked up a few things. I'll buckle this in if you want to see if any of that works."

She glanced in the first bag and was surprised to see a couple of pairs of jeans, a flannel Western-style shirt, a pair of hiking boots, a couple of sweatshirts and a thick-lined denim jacket. She checked the sizes. 2T. She'd guess that would be correct. That was fast. Rhett must've just grabbed them off the shelves. In the last bag she found an array of breakfast bars, a sippy cup, a five-pack of metal cars and a small bottle of milk.

Rhett held out his hands. "Want me to put him in?"

Not really, but she agreed Levi's safety outweighed the need to cuddle the toddler. She handed him over, Levi barely stirring. "Here you go."

Brandi had forgotten how tender Rhett could be. Even though they lived in the same county, she avoided the stores and restaurants Rhett frequented like the plague. Most days consisted of work, and then going home. She only went out when necessary. The suspicion she'd been treated with by lifelong neighbors and other people in town had been painful, but Rhett's lack of support had been the final knife to her heart. No matter how help-ful he seemed to be, she couldn't allow herself to get too close or concern herself with anything but keeping Levi safe and finding Sadie.

Rhett put the boy into the seat, careful not to wake him. He hoped he hadn't gone overboard with the clothes, but he wouldn't tolerate the little guy being cold. When he was a kid, more than once he had gone without a coat or clothes that fit. After his dad had abandoned his mom and family, food had been scarce. As long as Rhett was around, an innocent child would not go hungry or cold.

The situation reminded him of way too many cases he'd worked of single moms struggling to survive on a low income, or parents more concerned with their next high than their children.

Rhett climbed into the driver's seat, put the truck in gear and pulled out. "Did I do okay on the sizes?"

"Surprisingly, yeah. When did you become so knowledgeable on kids?"

He let the comment slide as he stopped at a red light, not wanting to point out that if Levi's mom—whether she turned out to be Sadie or not—abandoned the child in dangerous cold weather, there was a good chance the authorities would put him into a foster home. "Has anything recently happened that made you think your sister was alive?"

She broke eye contact and looked out her window. "If you mean besides Sadie's phone call, no."

The light turned green, and he accelerated, keeping one eye on his rearview mirror. The growing pink in the sky had the town awaking with Saturday morning's early risers. Houses were adorned with Christmas lights and blow-up decorations in their yards. "Tell me what's been going on in your life lately. Say, the last two weeks."

"You've got to be kidding me. Nothing out of the norm unless you count Mom got married to Phillip Sandford last week—at the courthouse of all places—but I'm sure you knew that." A touch of sarcasm laced her tone. "I worked five days this past week, two of which were double shifts because one of the dispatchers was out with the flu."

"Have you met anyone new?"

She sighed. "No one."

"Anything different at work?"

She shook her head. "Nothing."

Hostility radiated from Brandi, but Rhett didn't want to see her get her hopes up just to have them shattered again. She had to face the facts, good or bad. "It makes no sense. If Sadie's alive, where has she been the last two years? Why wouldn't she let everyone know she's all right, especially her family?"

Brandi rolled her shoulder, evidently trying to ease the tension. "Can't we discuss this after we listen to the call?"

"Sure. Just know there's a lot of unanswered questions that we need to investigate."

A few minutes later, they pulled into the parking lot, and Brandi hurried out of the truck and around to get Levi from his car seat. Rhett stepped out but gave her plenty of space. Her intenseness was obvious, and he knew not to crowd her. The temperatures were still cold enough to make them hurry inside.

Hoping to prove Sadie had made that call must be difficult for Brandi. He prayed she would accept the truth if the voice turned out to be someone else.

"Come on in." Shannon Woolsey, the dispatch supervisor, greeted them as they entered the door. Her medium-layered bob accentuated her no-nonsense demeanor. "I have the recording queued in my office where you can have privacy."

Shannon's gaze momentarily landed on Levi before she glanced at Brandi. She motioned for them to follow her. From the stories his uncle had told, Rhett knew the supervisor had been a superb police officer for over twelve years before sustaining a life-threatening injury during a domestic call. He wasn't aware of the extent of Shannon's wounds, but after she recovered, she was put in charge of dispatch services and was known to be a good leader who cared about her team.

Also, he'd heard she was one of the few in Mulberry Gap who didn't treat Brandi with suspicion.

"I listened to the recording again earlier, and at 3.2 seconds, I'm afraid there's not much to go on." Shannon indicated the computer. "I'll leave you two alone so you can listen. Let me know if you need anything." She slipped out of the room and closed the door.

Brandi sat in the blue cushioned chair with Levi in her arms. The tyke clung to her neck, and she pulled her hair free from his grasp. She slid one of the fruit-filled bars from her purse. "Here you go. Are you hungry?"

The boy didn't say anything but grabbed the food and stuffed a big bite in his mouth.

"Whoa, little guy." Rhett broke off a piece of the bar and set the other half on the edge of Shannon's exquisitely clean desk. Levi crammed it into his mouth, but at least he wouldn't choke now.

Brandi sent Rhett a half smile. "Thanks. I should've known not to hand him the whole bar."

Seeing his ex-fiancée's pale complexion and knowing the stress she was under to prove it was Sadie's voice on the call, he hoped they received answers quickly. Brandi had always been a tough one, and he didn't like seeing her vulnerable. Rhett liked to think that if she hadn't closed everyone off, he could've helped her heal.

Levi continued to eat, and Rhett noticed Brandi's hand tremble as she handed the boy another bite. No doubt uncertainty overwhelmed her thoughts. "Sadie has to be alive." Her words came out as a whisper.

"You've got your hands full. I'll do it." He hated the thought of her hopes being dashed and was ready to find out whose voice was on that recording.

She nodded but didn't say a word.

He hit the button.

"911. Wha—"

"The farm. Plea—" There was a shuffling in the background and the call went dead.

"That's her." She looked up at Rhett.

He narrowed his gaze, not convinced it was Brandi's younger sister on the recording. Maybe…

"The farm. Plea—"

This time, Levi reached out for the monitor.

"See."

Rhett shook head. "I don't know. It sounds like Sadie, but it's just too short."

As soon as the words were out of his mouth, Brandi's shoulders dropped and her lips pressed tight, alerting him he should've waited to voice his opinion.

"You've got to be kidding me." Brandi climbed to her feet, the chair screeching across the tile floor. "That's Sadie. Who else would say *the farm* and then leave her child at my grandparents'? Only someone who knew I'd understand. It's the only thing that makes sense."

"Or someone who knew your family. I'd say most people in Mulberry Gap know the farm and it's not exactly a unique name."

It wasn't what Rhett said as much as his stubborn expression that told Brandi she had expected too much by hoping he'd be on her side. *Trust him.* Yeah, whatever.

Surely the old argument if her sister was still alive would not be rekindled. Would anyone believe her? Probably not. Fine. She would find Sadie on her own. It was not like she had needed anyone for the last two years.

She couldn't stop her voice from shaking. "Believe me or not, that was Sadie. She's in trouble and I'm going to help her."

"Brandi…"

She marched out of the office. When she saw Shannon, she slowed. "Thank you. I really appreciate you letting us come in and listen to the tape." Rhett moved in behind her, but Brandi kept her back to him, as cold as a block of ice. "Have you heard any word on Deputy Norris?"

"Nothing since he was airlifted to Dallas. I'll let you know if we get an update." Shannon kept her eyes on her. The supervisor had to notice the tension even though Brandi tried to control her emotions. Dispatch and first responders communicated often between departments, so Shannon would be one of the first to hear about Norris's condition.

Rhett stepped close and his gaze collided with hers before he pivoted to Shannon. "Thank you, ma'am."

"You're welcome, Rhett."

Brandi refrained from rolling her eyes. Shannon had always encouraged her to give Rhett another chance. But her boss didn't understand how much she had begged for his assistance in finding Sadie. He'd insisted Sadie's case wasn't under his jurisdiction but rather that of the Jarvis County Sheriff's Department. Why didn't he or anyone simply help?

"Thanks, boss." Brandi headed toward the door with Rhett on her heels, and even though she didn't look at them, she figured all the dispatchers were staring at her.

No doubt day shift had heard about the call and her running out to meet her sister. But Brandi didn't have time to worry about gossip.

"Would you wait up?"

Brandi opened the back door of Rhett's truck and started buckling Levi in.

"You didn't have to march out like that. I'm on your side."

After getting Levi secured, she shut the door and climbed into the passenger side. "Take me to the farm."

"I'm on your side," he repeated.

Internally, she was shaking. "Look. I know you didn't want to help me when Sadie first went missing. No one did. Let me just do this on my own. Now take me to the farm."

Rhett put the truck into gear and pulled out of the drive. If it weren't for his knuckles turning white on the steering wheel, she might not have realized how irritated he was. But she'd known him a long time and recognized the simmer. The big breakup fight was one of the few times she'd witnessed an outburst of emotions.

He turned the truck right.

"Where are you going? I said I wanted to go back to my grandparents' place." She could call Shannon to come pick her up after she had time to look in her grandpa's truck again to make certain nothing was left that might tell her where Sadie had gone.

With an even voice, he said, "If you don't want to be questioned by the sheriff's department, you need to stay away until they clear out. I'll run by and take a look."

She sighed. Of course, investigators would be there processing the scene for evidence. "Take me to my mom's house, then." For good measure, she added, "Please."

"You sure you wouldn't feel safer at Pam's house?"

"Thanks, but I'd rather be at my mom's." Pam was Rhett's younger sister, a childcare worker by day and a self-defense instructor by night. Pam had always been friendly, but Brandi intended to take her mom's car to look for Sadie. Her sister wouldn't leave her son and go far away.

"Brandi, I don't mind helping you and Levi. If Sadie is still alive, I want to find her. I'll admit it sounded like her on the call, but we need to be certain. Where has she been?"

"You've already asked me that question and my answer is the same. I don't know."

He glanced in the rearview mirror. She assumed he was looking at Levi. Brandi drew a deep breath. Rhett truly was trying to help, and maybe she was a tad on edge. Okay. A lot on edge. She didn't like feeling bitter toward others, but she didn't like feeling as if she were backed into a corner, either. It caused her to come out fighting, like she was having to battle alone every step. "I don't know what happened to my sister. But it had to be important for her to leave so soon after Daddy died and never to call or come home. She had a baby. Why not come home? I'm an aunt. Mom is a grandma. Sadie would never keep her child from us unless there was a good reason."

Their last conversation had been a heated one, though. She and Sadie had fought more than usual the year before her disappearance. Brandi remembered looking forward to her sister getting out of the teen years to where they could have a normal discussion without getting into an argument. Her blood ran cold. Surely Sadie hadn't avoided coming home because of her?

Rhett turned on the county highway that led to her mom's house. "I want you to be realistic in case the caller was not Sadie."

"Like I live in a dream world?" No one had their feet more firmly planted on the ground than she. Brandi had to bite her lip not to say anything. She wasn't going to argue, but after hearing the call again, she was more convinced than ever that it had been her sister on the phone.

Was hope wrong?

Rhett gave her a look but chose to ignore her comment. A few minutes later, he pulled into her mom's drive. They brought Levi, the car seat and the clothes into the house. Since there would be food in the house, she left the snacks Rhett brought in his truck.

After a quick walk-through to make certain no one had been in the house, Rhett turned to her. His hands went up like he was going to rest them on her shoulders, but then he dropped them back to his side. To her chagrin, a part of her wouldn't have minded his support. But she wasn't that girl anymore.

"Lock up and call me if you need anything," he said. "I'll let you know what I learn."

"Thanks Rhett." She shut the door behind him and waited until his truck disappeared down the street before she loaded the car seat into her mom's Lexus RX SUV—a gift from her new husband. After grabbing binoculars and the car keys from the desk drawer, she put Levi into the vehicle. He awoke during the shuffle, but his eyes were closed again by the time she backed out of the garage.

The heater had warmed in no time, making the vehicle toasty. Brandi had never driven a luxury vehicle and would've preferred her mom's practical base-model

Hyundai, but Phil Sandford had insisted his wife drive something more *becoming*. Maybe Brandi was being petty, but it really irked her that Phil insinuated her mom's car, clothes and house weren't good enough. Like her father hadn't provided well for his wife.

After several miles through town, she turned down the country road leading to the farm. She had no intentions of interrupting the investigation, because Rhett was right—now wasn't the time to be questioned.

Sadie had to be close by. If Brandi was at the sheriff's office for any period of time, she might miss her opportunity to hear from her sister.

As she neared her grandparents' place, she slowed and noticed there were still at least three vehicles parked out front, including Rhett's truck. She kept her speed down as her gaze continued to search her surroundings for signs that a vehicle had gone through a neighboring pasture. Her real mission was to check out the small tin shed at the far back corner of the farm, approachable from the road, but from where a person could see the house across the fields. If Levi were her child and she had to leave in a hurry, Brandi would park under that shed and watch to make certain Levi had been taken care of.

She turned north a half mile down the road. A glance in her rearview mirror told her Levi was still asleep. As she approached the shed, she saw that knee-high dead grass filled the entry. She turned in but couldn't detect any tire tracks, and the ground was too muddy to pull in all the way.

Disappointment hit her. If someone had parked in here, there would be deep ruts. The grass made it difficult to tell, but there seemed to be no indication of recent activity. Her head dropped to the side. *Where did you go, Sadie?*

She grabbed her binoculars and peered through them. Only half the Victorian house was visible due to a limb overhanging the shed. She looked over her shoulder at Levi. The poor fellow was too exhausted to get out in this weather and the shed was only ten yards away. Leaving the car running with the heat on, she shrugged into her coat and stepped out into the deep grass. Due to recent rain, her shoe sank into the half-frozen mud.

Ah. No doubt Mom wouldn't appreciate her new car getting dirty, but too late now. Cold wind hit her, and she drew the jacket tighter. Another peek through the binoculars and she had a clear view of the house and buildings. Two men stood in the drive and another walked around the barn. The one by the barn would be Rhett—his long stride made him easily recognizable. Everyone who came and went could be observed. She trudged toward the backside of the shed. Light tire marks suddenly emerged. Had she been wrong? She turned back and stared at the ground again, a tilt of her head giving her a better look with her damaged eye. A gust of wind blew the grass and suddenly she could see it—a wide tire track. It couldn't be a heavy vehicle, or it would've been deeper.

She rounded the corner and found an ATV parked under the shed.

Adrenaline rushed through her veins. "Sadie? Are you here?"

Before questions of how Sadie could've driven the four-wheeler with Levi penetrated Brandi's brain, a rustle in the grass had her spinning around.

She caught the blur of a brown shirt on her weak side, and then a thick board swung high into the air. Her arms instinctively jerked to cover her head, but pain exploded in her skull and lights flashed before her eyes. She fell.

A deep voice mumbled, "One down and one to go."

Levi! She had to protect the baby. She crawled forward, the ground spinning as she attempted to get to her feet.

A powerful blow came down on her back and she crumpled. Then cold blackness.

FOUR

Rhett continued to look at the grounds while the deputies huddled in a small group outside the barn, complaining about the shooting of Deputy Norris and tossing around names of potential suspects. Brandi seemed to be at the top of the list. He tried to ignore them, but occasionally a word or statement carried his way.

The large Victorian house stood on a slight rise, no doubt giving an awesome view from the upper story. A long strand of Christmas lights dangled from the third floor. Estelle Callahan, Brandi's grandmother, had gone into the assisted-living facility right before Christmas last year and she must've been prepping for the holidays. December 25 was fast approaching, and the house once again would sit quiet and empty. It was a shame to see the old home falling into disrepair.

When he and Brandi dated, they had enjoyed several family get-togethers in this house. As much as Rhett tried to move on with his life, regret still plagued him. The double tornadoes had been disastrous for so many in the area, and several people were injured, but thankfully no lives had been lost. Unless you counted the Callahan family.

He needed to clear his mind and see if he could find clues as to who had attacked her and the deputy this morning. Why was the deputy at the farm in the first place? Did he know Brandi would be there? Or was he expecting someone else?

Brandi said she had run into the house with Levi and then the gunman raced upstairs. It was possible the man had left evidence behind in his haste to find her. Rhett strode forward, intent on examining the home when something glistened across the pasture.

He squinted. An automobile sat next to the old shed. Could it be the gunman's? The question no more had crossed his mind when he realized the vehicle was Brandi's mom's SUV.

His heart plunged into this stomach. He hurried across the yard to his truck. What was Brandi doing out here? He gritted his teeth. He'd warned her to stay at her mother's. He should've known she wouldn't listen. Brandi's desire to find Sadie overrode her common sense. The deputies stared as he sped by them and out the drive.

Flying down the rock road, he kept his gaze near the shed. Did something just move outside? At this distance he couldn't be certain. When he got to the drive, he whipped his truck behind the Lexus, grabbed his Glock and jumped out. The SUV was still running, and Levi was asleep, buckled in the back seat.

A low hum mingled in the frosty morning.

Suddenly there was the rumble of an engine and an ATV flew out from behind the shed. An average-size man wearing a brown shirt and a camouflage ski mask held on to the handlebar with one hand and a gun with the other. The machine headed straight for Rhett. Not knowing where Brandi was, Rhett didn't fire his weapon.

He lunged in front of the Lexus to keep the target away from Levi as bullets riddled the ground. The man moved too fast to aim accurately.

Rhett jumped to his feet. He lifted his Glock and fired twice, but the man disappeared behind the brush that lined the road. The engine faded into the distance.

He ran around the side of the shed. "Brandi!" At first glance, Rhett didn't see her, but then his eyes locked onto something.

Brandi's body slumped on the grass.

His breath hitched as he moved to her side. Dirt and mud caked the back of her head and a dark smudge crossed her back. A board lay on the ground beside her. "Brandi." He kneeled and felt for a pulse. A low but steady thump was a welcome response. Careful not to move her in case she had other injuries, he said, "Wake up."

She stirred and her face wrinkled into a frown. "What? Rhett?" Her gaze locked onto his, confusion evident as she tried to sit. "Levi!"

"He's fine."

"No." She shoved his hands away and struggled to her feet. "There's a man…"

"The man is gone. Levi is fine."

"You can't know that." She was almost in hysterics.

"Brandi, come look." Taking her hand to make sure she didn't fall on the rough ground, he led her to the SUV.

Her hands went to her chest. "I'm so glad. I was petrified the man was going to take Levi. He hit me over the head with a board."

Rhett wanted to scold her for coming out here alone, but he decided to let Brandi get her bearings first. "You're freezing. Let's get you inside the warm vehicle."

She readily agreed and climbed in on the driver's side. Rhett went to the passenger's side.

They had no more shut the doors than a little voice came from the back seat. "Hungee."

They both turned around. Brandi smiled. "You can have anything you want."

Considering how relieved she was Levi was unharmed, Rhett figured that was true. He might even agree. Realization of how easily the man could've hurt or killed both Brandi and Levi hit a little too close to home.

Without thought, he said, "The man had a gun and shot at me. Don't leave without telling me where you're going again." He realized his mistake as soon as her lips flattened, and her eyebrows arched. "I didn't mean that—"

"Don't tell me what to do. I've made it fine by myself the last two years without anyone's help." Her face burned red.

"Brandi, you scared me when I realized that was your mom's vehicle in the pasture. I wish you had told me. It won't do any good if we find your sister, but you die in the process." He realized she knew this, and she had always been a smart and responsible lady. She even had law enforcement training. But her determination could be her undoing. "Did you recognize the man?"

"No." She grabbed the back of her head and cringed. "Everything happened too fast."

"How bad is the pain?"

"It's throbbing, but I'm okay."

"Let me see your eyes."

She lifted her chin and stared at him.

"They're slightly dilated." He reached over and touched her head. Even though he tried to be gentle, she flinched.

"You've got a knot." He tilted his head as he scrutinized her. "You need to be checked out."

"No." The word came out loud, almost panicked. She brought down her tone a bit. "Please. I'm fine. If it gets worse, I'll go get checked out."

He shook his head even though he understood the temptation to refuse medical treatment. "You were knocked out. We need to make certain you don't have a concussion."

"I couldn't have been out for long since you said you saw the man. And I know the signs of concussion. I give instructions every day to injured people before the first responders arrive."

Daily, she did help people with an array of problems, but that didn't mean she was a nurse or doctor. Again, he felt the bump. Knots on the head tended to come up fast, but also healed quickly. He examined her yet again. Her eyes were not quite as dilated.

"Come on. Quit looking at me like that. I'm not fragile and you know it. If the shoe were on the other foot, there's no way you'd go to the hospital. We need to find out the man's identity and quit wasting time sitting here. If I get to feeling bad, I'll go in."

He didn't like it, but he intended on keeping a close eye on her. "I'll hold you to your word."

Brandi had always been afraid to show weakness, but he imagined she was even worse after everything she had been through. He asked her, "Did you get a good look at the man?"

"Like I said, not really. Maybe he had on a mask? Like the ones people wear to go hunting. And a brown shirt."

Rhett also hadn't got a good look and didn't want to

ask his next question. "Was the shirt the same color as the sheriff's department uniform?"

"Yeah, maybe. I hate to ask this, but you said the man shot at you. How come he hit me with a board if he had a gun?"

That question had gone through Rhett's mind, too. "He was probably afraid gunfire would call the attention of the investigators at the farm. I left him no choice and he had to fire his weapon to escape."

"That makes sense."

Deputy Zdeb pulled up and walked over to Rhett's side. He was forty-something with a potbelly and was one of the deputies working the scene at the farm. Rhett didn't know much about him except he'd transferred from south Texas a year ago.

Rhett rolled down the window.

"Everything all right, Kincaid? I heard shots fired."

"Someone hit Brandi over the head a few minutes ago and then the man shot at me as he got away."

Distrust exuded from the man's expression, but he reined it in. "Are you all right, ma'am? Do you need paramedics?"

"No. I'm fine." Brandi sat straight as if to prove her point.

Rhett asked, "Did any of the deputies leave the scene?"

The man squinted. "What are you trying to insinuate?"

Rhett didn't believe in playing games, especially with other law officers. "I'm not insinuating anything. But you and the other deputies were talking up Brandi being Norris's shooter. Did anyone leave the crime scene before I arrived?"

"I'm under no obligation to answer your questions,

Ranger. But no one left." He glanced across the vehicle to Brandi. "Are you sure you're okay?"

"Yes."

Rhett got out of the SUV. "Come on. I'll show you." He didn't want to talk to the deputy, but he'd have to deal with his uncle if he withheld information, and he didn't relish the thought of that.

Doubt that he could protect Brandi scared him more than he cared to admit. One thing was certain: somebody knew to check out the shed and had brought an ATV in preparation.

Brandi waited with Levi in the warmth of the vehicle while Deputy Zdeb and Rhett checked out the shed. She assumed Rhett was filling him in on what happened.

Her head and back still throbbed. Tears of frustration pooled in her eyes, but she squeezed them back. She hated weakness. Hated relying on others. But she'd been terrified the man would take Levi and was relieved Rhett had shown up in time to run the man away. That was twice in one day her ex had saved her.

She tried to recall the man's features, but the attack had happened so quickly it was a blur. The color brown seemed to be prominent. The shade could be that of the sheriff's department clothes or hunting gear. Or maybe the guy simply liked brown. Why did he want to hurt her? Did he think she had seen something?

The pain in her head grew worse the more she concentrated, but not enough to go to the emergency room. Mom always carried a first aid kit. She glanced in the glove box but found only the owner's manual. She pulled out a white box of supplies under the passenger's seat.

When she got back to her mom's, she'd clean the injury and apply ointment.

Levi kicked his car seat. "Hungee."

She smiled and pointed to herself. "Brandi will get you something to eat. Rhett is hurrying. It'll be a minute." Of course, Levi wouldn't know what a minute meant, but she didn't know how to explain time to a toddler. His brown eyes glistened as he stared at her and her heart melted. She'd totally forgotten about the snacks Rhett had purchased earlier in the day. "Brandi will be right back."

Leaving the door open, she got out and grabbed the sack of food from the back seat of Rhett's truck. Her head throbbed with the movement.

When she got back in, she unwrapped the variety snack pack and gave Levi a couple of small squares of cheese. He stuffed a slice in his mouth. Suddenly, she wondered if he was allergic to dairy. Maybe she shouldn't have given him the cheese. She didn't know anything about him. They needed to learn more about Sadie's child. Did he have any medical conditions? Did he still take a pacifier? A bottle? He had taken the sippy cup earlier, so she guessed he was fine drinking without a bottle. He hadn't had a diaper bag, but Sadie could've been in such a hurry she'd forgotten some of his things.

Just like she had left his stuffed teddy bear in her car. At least she had his blanket.

Brandi couldn't help but defend Sadie in her mind every time a negative thought surfaced. Even though Sadie had her problems, her little sister displayed a sweet disposition and had been a good girl. Her parents had raised them right.

Rhett and the deputy came out from around the shed,

and Rhett pointed to the farm. They were still deep in conversation as they stood there.

Her mind returned to Sadie and the last time she'd seen her sister. Sadie had gotten in late again, this time on a weeknight. Preoccupied with grief after losing her husband, Mom had spent most of her time locked in her room and had gone to bed early. Sadie was just seventeen, and Brandi had worried she was starting to go wild. Multiple times, her sister had missed curfew and tended to go out with kids who had less than stellar reputations. Her grades had dropped from high As to low Cs. Since Mom didn't step in, Brandi did. At first, she had simply tried to talk to her sister and encourage her. But when that didn't work, Brandi had become irritated and impatient.

That night, Sadie had gotten in well after midnight and Brandi met her at the door. Her sister's breath smelled of alcohol. She'd yelled at Sadie, demanding to know where she got the beer and told her it was illegal for anyone to buy it for her. Brandi had warned her sister that if Mom didn't do anything, she would tell Rhett and let him find out who was giving alcohol to minors.

That had set Sadie off. She'd screamed that Brandi wasn't her parent and she should mind her own business. The tirade ended with Sadie shrieking, "I hate you." Then she'd stormed into her room and slammed the door.

It was the last time Brandi had seen her. Brandi never told anyone Sadie's last words, not even Rhett.

Shame filled her and her throat went dry. Even though Brandi had good intentions, she had acted like a child herself. If only she could have a do-over, she would be more patient. In retrospect, she should have tried to get her help and listened, instead of lecturing. A grief counselor might've helped.

Had there been more going on in Sadie's life? Besides anger, had fear driven her sister's outburst? Had Sadie been in danger back then?

Rhett and the deputy started walking toward the vehicles.

Rhett slid into the SUV, and the deputy got into his own vehicle. "I made the report. Is there anything else you can tell me about the man?"

"Not really. When I saw the tire tracks, my mind was so preoccupied with finding Sadie near the shed that I let my guard down. I saw a blur of movement and then he hit me on the head."

"Was it the same bearded guy you saw this morning?"

"I don't think so. This one was smaller."

"He didn't look to have a big build to me, either," Rhett said. "Did he say anything?"

"No." Suddenly the man's words came back to her. "Wait. Yes. After he hit me, he said, 'One down and one to go.'"

Her gaze locked with Rhett's. Fear for Sadie tightened around her neck like a noose. "He plans to kill both of us."

FIVE

Frustration and fear clawed at Rhett. The man on the ATV had made it clear he intended to get rid of Sadie and Brandi. But why? According to Brandi, this man was smaller than the bearded one from this morning, who'd shot Deputy Norris and run her off the road in the Bronco.

Two men. Someone must've paid them. Which made Rhett believe the attacks had to do with the missing money. Whoever took the money believed the girls knew something or knew something to incriminate him or them. Did the two men steal the money, or were they being paid by someone else?

"Let's return your mom's vehicle back to her house and you can ride with me. It's safer if we stay together."

"I'm fine." Her hand came up and she closed her eyes. When she opened them again, she said, "Never mind. You're right. For now."

Rhett followed in his truck as she drove the SUV back to her mom's and parked in the garage. Several minutes later, she and Levi were in his truck again as Rhett headed toward his house. Brandi had remained quiet during the drive, and he was thankful she didn't go off on her own. Levi kicked the back of the driver's seat and babbled words Rhett couldn't understand. Brandi had given the little guy two of the toy cars to play with.

Rhett drove around to the back of the house and out of sight in case someone pulled up. "I don't see any signs of intruders, but let me check out the place before you go in."

"Okay."

A quick walk-through turned up nothing. After helping Brandi bring Levi in, he performed another search of the outside of the property. Besides a bullet hole in his front porch post from the shooting this morning, everything was untouched.

As he walked through the door, Brandi asked, "So, what now?" She stood beside the dining table, her hands gripping the back of a chair.

"First, I'm going to call Lieutenant Adcock to let him know what's going on." He slid his gun back into his holster.

"We need to find Sadie."

"We will."

She frowned. "I can't just wait around."

"I wouldn't expect you to." Brandi struggled with patience. Not that he blamed her. He also needed to keep them safe, which meant they couldn't go running off without letting someone know their plans. "Let me make the call and then we'll talk. I'll be right back."

He didn't give her time to respond but strode to his bedroom and left the door cracked open. He hit his boss's number.

"Kincaid. You were supposed to check in this morning."

"I've been busy." Rhett gave him a rundown of the

day's events, from his initial chase, the shooting of the deputy at the farm, to the attack on Brandi at the shed.

Adcock listened until Rhett finished. "Brandi Callahan. How do I know that name?"

Rhett took a deep breath. He wasn't a rookie anymore, but he didn't need his boss to worry about a conflict of interest. "I tried to help Brandi find her sister a couple of years ago."

There was a moment of silence. "Wasn't the lady your girlfriend?"

"Yes, sir. My fiancée."

Again, a pause. "What's the current situation?"

He glanced over his shoulder to make sure Brandi wasn't standing by the door. "I hadn't seen her in two years until this morning." That didn't mean he hadn't thought about her or inquired about her well-being from mutual friends. He needed to be honest. His boss was a fair man and mild-mannered to a point. But the lieutenant didn't like to be left in the dark with information. "Sir, I plan to help her find her sister. It appears both women are in danger."

"This is not our jurisdiction. It should be under Jarvis County Sheriff's Department or the local police." The lieutenant's exact same response as two years ago.

"Yes, sir." Rhett couldn't let Brandi down again. He needed to be careful how he phrased his reply. "There is reason to believe the sheriff's department might be involved."

"That's a serious accusation."

"I'm not certain of anything, but I would appreciate the opportunity to find Sadie Callahan."

"Kincaid, you're a good Ranger. I don't have to tell

you how crucial this is. We can't officially investigate this case unless asked to do so."

"I'm aware of the situation. I can take a few days off, but I'd like to help Miss Callahan. She feels I let her down last time." Lieutenant Adcock was tough as nails, but he also had common sense and compassion—a rare trait these days.

"I'll give you three or four days. But Kincaid, I have confidence in you not to overstep your bounds. I expect no phone calls from local law enforcement."

Rhett smiled. "I understand and appreciate it."

"Keep me updated."

"Yes, sir." Rhett clicked off and turned around to see Levi standing in the open door.

Levi ran to him with his hands in the air. "'Ett."

Did the boy try to say his name? He hit himself in the chest with his finger. "Rhett."

Levi nodded. "'Ett."

A pang in his heart blindsided him at the boy's trust. Rhett was just a stranger, but the toddler had already come to depend on him and Brandi. He scooped him up and walked into the living room with the boy in his arms.

Brandi stood at the window, staring out to the front yard. Cartoons played on the television, the sound turned down low. She turned. "Oh, I'm sorry. I didn't notice he left the room."

"He hadn't. He was standing in the doorway. I'm sure he heard me talking."

She nodded. "I don't like to admit it, but I have no idea where to start. What do we do?"

"We continue to investigate while staying safe."

"Did your boss say anything? He didn't pull you off the case?"

Like last time. Brandi didn't say the words, but it was the underlying meaning. "No, but technically I'm not on the case. He warned me this wasn't the Texas Rangers' jurisdiction, but he agreed to let me have a few days off."

Her lips pressed together, and she nodded. The action shouted skepticism. "Okay."

"Brandi, I'm going to do everything I can. No matter if the lady on the call was or wasn't Sadie, or if Levi isn't her child, I won't stop until we find her."

"I can't believe you just said that. I thought we had moved past the question of the identity of the caller." She planted her hands on her hips.

He held his hand up. "I'm going to find out who is behind these attacks, but I deal with facts. I believe it's possible the female on the phone is your sister. I'm also open to it being someone else. Can we agree to work together to gather the information no matter the result? Let's find the truth together. Agreed?"

"It was Sadie on the phone. Levi is her son."

He shook his head. "Just the truth. Because if you're not ready to deal with facts, you'll purposely see what you want."

"Please," she said sarcastically. "I know you're not supposed to investigate with an agenda." She made quotes in the air. "Police training, remember? I don't think some stranger called 911 and then left her child at my grandparents' farm."

"Agreed?" He ignored her bait.

If a smile could have an attitude, Brandi's lips fit the bill. "Agreed. Now, how are we going to find Sadie?"

He shook his head. "You're stubborn."

"Thank you. It's a common trait with us Callahans."

"Down." Levi kicked his legs and Rhett set him on

the floor. The boy ran straight for his sippy cup and held it in the air.

Brandi walked into the kitchen. "Do you need more to drink?"

Levi stayed on her heels. "Mur."

She opened the refrigerator and removed the juice boxes Rhett had bought earlier.

Rhett sat on the couch and put in a call to Luke Dryden, a fellow Texas Ranger. Brandi paced the room and listened while keeping an eye on Levi. The little guy only halfway watched the cartoons while roaming the room and checking everything out. When Rhett was through talking with his coworker, he turned to her. "Give me your list of suspects."

She sat in the recliner across from him, covered up with the light blanket he'd kept on the back of the chair. She sat cross-legged and had her elbows propped on her knees. "You know I don't trust the sheriff's department."

Levi crawled into her lap.

"Which ones in particular?" He grabbed a yellow legal pad from the small built-in desk.

"All of them."

He lifted one eyebrow.

"I was questioned several times. By Norris. Coble. Your uncle, and a couple of others."

"The deputies who did the questioning are at the top of your list?"

She glanced toward the wall. "Not necessarily. It was more of a feeling someone had instructed them to point their investigation toward me."

"Were there any questions in particular that made you uncomfortable?"

"Yeah. We had this conversation two years ago when it was happening."

He smiled. "Humor me and repeat it, please."

"The fundamental question was, 'Did you take the money?' That one didn't settle well. And when I told them no, they asked if my dad was having money problems and if he had come into a lot of money lately. A look into my parents' bank account should have answered that. Of course, I answered with a resounding no."

Rhett was sure she did. This would not be easy because she was too defensive. Before he could form a response, she continued.

"And please don't tell me how that's normal protocol. I realize those are typical questions. And suspects can be questioned for hours on end. It wasn't so much that I was questioned or what they asked. More like what they wouldn't do. Like look at someone else besides my family, because they'd made up their minds we were guilty. Especially my dad."

"How do you know they didn't look at others?"

"Every time I mentioned they needed to look elsewhere, I got the same response. 'Your dad oversaw the fund.' It was like they were determined my dad stole the money and our family had buried it in the backyard."

He had to wonder if the department checked other people and Brandi simply didn't know about it. "Did you make suggestions for other suspects?"

"Yes. Phil Sandford, now my mom's husband." She rolled her eyes. "And all the other bank employees."

Phillip Sandford would be a legitimate suspect. He should've been interviewed. He jotted his name on the paper. "Anyone else at the bank?"

She shrugged. "Everyone with access to the account.

It took two employees to access the account unless you were high up in the bank. Supposedly that was only my dad and Phil, but what if someone else hacked the bank's computer and accessed it? Someone who lost everything in the tornado or someone from out of the area—even out of the country—that was good with computers?"

"That's a good question, and I'm assuming the FBI checked the computers."

"Did they check?" She gave an exaggerated shrug. "I don't know. Even the FBI seemed to mainly concentrate on my family."

"Did your dad have any enemies?"

"Of course not." She scowled. "Everyone liked him."

"If that were true and he didn't steal the money, then who did? Anyone who took the money would know it would point back to your dad."

"I don't know." She folded her arms across her chest. "Isn't that why we're making this list?"

"What about Sadie?"

Brandi went still. "What about her?"

"Did they question you about her?"

"A little. And when I suggested someone could've kidnapped Sadie because they mistakenly thought she had the money, your uncle actually laughed."

Not a professional response, but that didn't mean the sheriff's department or FBI didn't investigate the lead. Because Rhett was with the Texas Rangers, he hadn't had access to the files. Maybe now his uncle would help him, but Rhett would have to handle this delicately.

"Do you believe Sadie was in on the theft?"

"What?" Her voice grew loud. "No. Of course not."

Levi looked up at Brandi, a frown firmly in place.

Her tone turned playful, and she gave the boy a gentle squeeze. "It's okay, Levi. Brandi will talk quieter to Rhett." After he looked back to the cartoons, she sent Rhett a dirty look.

Even though she denied the likelihood of Sadie being involved, he knew the possibility must've crossed her mind. "Right. But remain open to the facts."

She started to open her mouth when Levi dropped his cup on the floor.

Rhett picked it up and set it on the coffee table. Brandi repositioned the little fellow on her lap and covered him with the blanket before sending another glare his way.

He turned his attention back to the suspects. "Anyone else to put on my list?"

"I keep going back to Dad's funeral." Brandi rubbed her head.

Rhett waited patiently for her to continue. He remembered the memorial like it was yesterday. The tiny church building had been packed. Not surprising, considering Mulberry Gap was a small town, and most citizens knew Jordan Callahan. But Rhett had noticed the unusual hush over the crowd. As if people were anticipating the family's reaction or expected something big to be revealed.

After a few songs and a couple of speeches, the event was over, and people had dispersed and gone home, disappointment on some faces. Several officers from the sheriff's department had attended, including his uncle. Understandably, Brandi's mom's eyes had been puffy from crying, but Brandi had always been subdued in showing her emotions. Sadie had been stoic, almost in shock, her face pale. No tears.

Like she carried guilt.

Everyone handled grief differently, and Sadie had still

been a teenager—he could understand the odd reaction and didn't mention it.

He recalled the Callahan house being searched when Sadie disappeared, but investigators had found nothing except for her purse and cell phone, which caused them to believe someone might have abducted her. After a few weeks, authorities had concluded she was probably dead, assuming she would've returned home if she was alive.

"Why don't we go back to your mom's house and this time we'll check it out."

"For what?" Hope sprang to Brandi's voice. "I've gone through the house several times. Mom and Phil are not home. Remember?"

"That's why I think it's a good time to visit."

New appreciation developed in her smile.

SIX

Loading a toddler and making sure she had his coat, snacks, diapers and wipes took more time than Brandi had realized. She'd heard coworkers complain but couldn't relate until now. She glanced over her shoulder.

Levi held his blanket in one hand and a blue sports car toy in the other while he stared out the window.

"I'd like to buy him some toys and a few more clothes for Christmas," she said.

Rhett glanced at her before looking back to the road. "What was that look for?"

He shook his head. "Nothing."

He didn't have to say it. Brandi knew what he was thinking. *Don't get too attached.* Well, Levi had already grown on her. How could you not love an innocent child? Children were ten times more trustworthy than adults.

"To make you happy, I should add I'd like to buy him things for Christmas no matter whose child he is."

Rhett's mouth twisted into a smirk, and he shook his head.

She wasn't going to worry about what he thought. A ding sounded and she glanced at her cell. A text from Shannon.

Wanted to give you update. Deputy Norris is out of surgery. Took nine hours. The doctor put him in a medically-
induced coma until his vitals become stable. Will let you
know if I hear anything more.

Brandi relayed the message to Rhett. She tried to read
his facial expression, but it was blank. "What? What are
you thinking?"

He shook his head. "I know it's been less than, what,
thirteen hours since he was shot? But I pray Norris pulls
through."

The statement was loaded with implications. Not only
was Norris a family man, but if he died, the sheriff's
department would be more determined to put his killer
behind bars. And to Brandi's knowledge, the list of suspects was a short one.

She'd been so busy thinking about her sister, she
hadn't thought much about the deputy. "Why did Norris pull a gun on me at farm? I was at my grandparents'
place and wasn't doing anything illegal."

Rhett glanced at her. "I don't know. How long after
you arrived did Norris show up?"

"Just a few minutes. Ten, fifteen minutes tops." Brandi
stared at him. "It's a good twenty minutes from the sheriff's department to the farm. How did he get there so
quickly?"

"Maybe he was already in the area." Rhett shrugged.
"Out on another call."

The confused looked on Norris's face played through
her mind. "Deputy Norris did a double take at the gunman like he hadn't expected to see him. But what or who
did he believe he'd find when he arrived?"

"You mean like he already knew you were at the

farm… Not a call from a neighbor driving home late at night and reporting a break-in or something."

She nodded. "Yeah. Like he was sent there to arrest me. He called me by name."

Rhett's eyes narrowed. "It was dark outside, and you were running."

"Yeah." She continued to nod. "Doubtful he could identify me that quickly."

"Possible, but not likely. He may've recognized your vehicle."

"True. But why pull a gun on me?" Her head hurt with the implications. "I was no threat, and I had every right to be there."

"I don't know. We have a lot more questions than answers."

And everything led back to Sadie's 911 call.

A few minutes later, they pulled up to her mom's place. Straight rows of clear lights lined the roof of the modest brick house. No doubt Phil hadn't climbed on a ladder but hired a professional company. A large plain wreath hung on the front door.

Blah and boring, if you asked her.

What did Mom do with those multicolored sets that flashed to the beat of Christmas music, which Dad had hung up for ten years? And the old Santa's sleigh Dad had put on top of the house that cars used to line up for blocks to behold? Was it in the attic or had Phil gotten rid of the family heirloom?

She'd like to have the sleigh if it were still around.

"Are you ready to go in or do you want to scowl at the house a little longer?"

She turned her attention to the man beside her. "Ha ha. Not funny." Even though she fought the feeling, Phil

Sandford's touch on her childhood home ate her up with annoyance. It would've been easier to swallow if he and her mom had moved into his old home. Of course, Phil's ex-wife, Gloria, had taken the house and the three kids along with the family poodle.

Rhett grabbed Levi from the back seat. "I know this is your mom's house, but I must warn you, we can't remove anything without their permission."

She'd always been welcome in her parents' home and didn't appreciate the thought of being considered an intruder. But she agreed and then they went inside.

If Rhett noticed a difference in the home, he didn't say so. He put Levi down and the boy ran straight into the living room for the new glass ornament sitting on the hearth.

"Wait." Brandi chased after him, but Levi was too fast. He picked up the fragile figurine of the nutcracker, and when he saw Brandi coming, his eyes grew large with panic. It slipped from his hands and shattered on the tile.

His lip puckered, and he ran to the recliner. "Saw-ree."

"It's okay." She playfully patted him on the head so he wouldn't think he was in trouble. "I'll clean it up. It was an accident."

Levi's big brown eyes stayed glued to her as she smiled and went into the kitchen.

"Why don't you let me watch him? The house is not babyproofed for a boy his age." Rhett swung Levi up on his shoulders.

Levi grinned, and his fingers grabbed hold of Rhett's short hair. It surprised her the Ranger's hair was long enough to get a good hold, but Levi managed. A laugh escaped her as Rhett cringed.

"The boy has an outstanding grip." Rhett smiled—sorta.

She swept up the broken glass and threw it into the trash. Brandi didn't recognize the nutcracker, so it must've been new.

"The little guy and I are going to look around if that's okay."

"Fine by me. Phil's office is back there." She pointed. "Nothing else has changed."

"I wouldn't say that. If it's any consolation, I remember your parents' and your grandparents' homes during the holidays. Your family blessed me by treating me like part of the family, and your home had that everyone-is-welcome feeling."

Rhett headed down the hall to the room that had once been her dad's. Brandi barely kept her mouth from falling open and hoped he didn't detect the awkwardness. Their last Christmas together he'd kissed her—not just any kiss, but a bend-her-backward-until-she-squealed kind of kiss—under the mistletoe in this very room in front of family. Ever the private one, Brandi had blushed with embarrassment as everyone laughed.

Deep sadness seeped into her bones at what all they'd lost. Not just her, but her dad, her mom, Grandma and Rhett. Even though Daddy had never voiced his opinion, Brandi knew he approved of Rhett and would've been proud to have him as a son-in-law.

Back at the beginning of their relationship, she'd been close to family and attending the police academy in the morning while working second shift in dispatch. Rhett had taught one of her investigative classes. She'd seen him in high school, but being several years younger than him, she hadn't gotten to know him until that class. They'd dated for over a year before he proposed.

A month later, the double tornado had hit town, followed by her father's death and the eye injury that ended her career in law enforcement before it even started.

She swallowed down the emotion. This was not the time to dwell on their past.

Brandi ignored the new furnishings in the living room and padded back to her old room. Shock slammed into her when she saw an electric guitar and other instruments leaning against the wall where her bed used to be. Her old bookcase now contained piles of sheet music instead of her old Nancy Drew and Hardy Boys books.

Where was her stuff?

She stalked to her closet door and flung it open. More of Phil's junk. An old letter jacket and camouflage coveralls hung on the rack, and a variety of fishing equipment filled the floor. A black trash bag, barely visible, sat in the back corner and contained some of her old clothes. Her mouth dropped open. Wasn't there room in the garage or attic for his things?

Sadie's room. Brandi made a beeline for her sister's room. Her chest tightened with each step. *So help me…*

She hurried through the door. Except for the room being clean, it was just as her sister left it. Relief flooded her as she released a breath.

The space looked like it was waiting for Sadie to walk back in and pick up where she'd left off. Their mom had rearranged the room, but most of her sister's things still decorated the dresser and walls. The posters of Sadie's favorite science fiction movie were gone, as well as the one of the eighteen-year-old teen idol she'd had a crush on. Besides the posters, everything else remained the same. Sadness encompassed her like a dark fog that wouldn't lift.

Brandi opened the top drawer of the dresser.

She had already gone through her sister's room right after her disappearance, hoping to find a clue. Rhett had also gone through her things, along with a couple of other investigators from the sheriff's department. At the time, it had felt like a violation, to see them handle Sadie's personal belongings as if they were their business. Brandi knew they must do their job, but it probably had more to do with them treating her family like suspects.

She didn't trust them.

Or anyone else except for Shannon and a couple of other people. Even her old high school classmates seemed to look at her oddly nowadays. Brandi had to admit, her life was lonely, as she rarely got together with friends anymore.

The top drawers contained underclothes. The next couple held a variety of things like T-shirts and shorts and swimsuits. There was nothing of value like a diary or a goodbye note that might give a clue as to what had happened to Sadie. Of course, Brandi couldn't help but pray now that she'd missed something valuable when she went through it the first few times.

When Brandi was a freshman in high school, she'd had a crush on Ryker Munson and didn't want anyone to know, so she had taped his picture underneath the nighttime drawer. Wondering if Sadie had done the same thing, she pulled out the dresser drawers and the two in the nightstand and checked. Nothing except for a dead spider and a couple of cobwebs. She sat on the twin bed and glanced around the room. A stuffed panda bear lay on her bed. Brandi picked it up and held it against her chest.

Sadie had just been a kid.

Brandi's chest grew heavy as she wondered if her kid sister were still alive. If she was, had she been through something terrible? The 911 call continued to replay through her head—the nervous voice, the sudden disconnection.

Could she have been alive these past two years only to be killed last night? The thought made her sick. *One down and one to go.* If so, the guy on the ATV didn't know about it.

Brandi needed to shove these thoughts aside. Sadie *had* to be alive.

She sighed and pushed to her feet. The closet door stood open, and a light denim jacket drew her attention. Sadie had worn that coat throughout the winter. Brandi removed it from the hanger and shrugged into it. Faint but still there, a strange odor came to Brandi. She drew it close and inhaled.

She jerked away. What was that?

It wasn't smoke, although Brandi figured Sadie had given cigarettes a try. It was some kind of perfume, but not feminine. That was it. It was a cheap cologne. She hadn't smelled it since high school when Noah Spalding sat beside her in Algebra. He was a quiet and nice guy, but his cologne used to send her allergies into overdrive. Whoever Sadie had been with must've used the same cheap brand.

Noah? Probably not, but it was something worth checking out.

She checked the compartments of the jacket. A movie ticket stub was in the right pocket and the left one was empty. She didn't think Sadie used the top pockets, but she slid her hand in there anyway.

Her finger touched paper.

Quickly, she removed and unfolded the note. A ring fell out and bounced across the carpet. She allowed the piece of jewelry to sit while she read. Scrawled across the middle of the paper, in Sadie's handwriting, was the date June 28 and an address. Realization hit Brandi. That was the week Sadie had disappeared. She quickly removed her cell from her back pocket and entered the address into the search box. Mulberry Women's Health Clinic.

The clinic performed pregnancy tests among other procedures. Brandi read the paper again to be certain she hadn't misunderstood.

Her attention went to the large silver ring on the floor. A guy's senior ring. She retrieved it and the bold letters MGHS stood out clearly. Mulberry Gap High School. The inscription on the inside read, "Wesley Alan Kincaid."

The sheriff's son? Brandi's eyes squeezed shut. Sadie had still been seeing Wes? Brandi thought they had quit dating months earlier.

"Did you find something?"

She jumped at the masculine voice. "Rhett, you scared me."

"Sorry." He stepped into the room with Levi at his feet.

She slid the ring and paper into the back pocket of her jeans. "Not much."

Rhett nodded, but continued to stare at her. "Are you certain you didn't find something?"

Should she tell him? With Wes being his cousin, Rhett would be tempted to tell his uncle. She returned the jacket to the closet. She wanted to trust Rhett, but if Wes had anything to do with Sadie's disappearance, she didn't want to chance Rhett warning his family. Brandi would be treated like an outsider again while the rest of the people banded together, making her mission to learn the truth nearly impossible.

"I'm going through Sadie's clothes. It's hard seeing and touching—even smelling her things. I recognize the odor on her jacket as the same cologne that Noah Spalding used to wear." None of that was a lie.

"Noah? I don't recall him."

"He was a quiet kid in my Algebra class. He had a younger brother named Blaze, in Sadie's class, but I don't remember them hanging out." At Rhett's nod, she wanted to get off the subject of what her search had turned up. "Did you find anything?"

Levi browsed the room and put his hands on everything. Brandi saw nothing he could hurt, so she allowed him to explore.

Rhett said, "Phil doesn't have many papers or documents in the office. Mainly books and typical office equipment. There was one thing, though."

She stood straight. "What?"

"A receipt dated last month for a fifty-thousand-dollar withdrawal from a bank. In and of itself, that's not suspicious. Phil may've invested well or been a stickler for saving his money. But the bank is in the Cayman Islands."

Brandi's mouth dropped open. "Seriously? Why would Phil need a foreign bank account?"

Rhett put his hands up and waved them down. "Don't make too much of it until we find out more. I took a picture of the receipt and sent it to Luke. He'll turn it over to our investigator with the Rangers. Hopefully, we should hear back in a day or two. If we can find out when the account was opened and how much money is in there, it could be a lead."

"That's the first good news I've heard." Her smile faded. "I hope Mom is okay. If my new stepfather was behind the theft, do you think she's in danger?"

"They're in Cozumel, right?"

She nodded. "Not supposed to be home until next Friday."

"If he's out of the country, someone here would have to be keeping him informed. Do you know anyone he's close to?"

She shrugged. "I haven't spent much time around him. He enjoys golf and I suppose he knows a lot of businessmen through the bank like my dad did."

"There weren't many things in the office. He probably hasn't moved all his things yet. Didn't he live in an apartment after the divorce?" At her nod, he continued. "Since he and your mom are not back from their honeymoon, I'd say most of his things are in his apartment."

"Waiting to get married didn't stop good ol' Phil from taking over my old bedroom. His guitar and other junk replaced all my things."

Rhett's dark eyes zoomed in on her. "I'm sorry, Brandi. It's tough—your dad dying and your mom moving on to another relationship…"

Not just any relationship. One with her dad's ex-coworker. She didn't say it aloud because Rhett was aware of the situation, and she didn't want to come off as being petty. Frustration bit at her. She intended to restore her family's reputation, and the chances she'd be fighting against the Kincaid family seemed inevitable.

But if Phil were the one who stole the fund, the Kincaids would be in the clear.

She watched Rhett as he scooped Levi into his arms and withdrew the red Hot Wheels truck that came from the value pack. Levi snatched it up.

Their relationship had ended, but they'd never been enemies. She prayed her gut feeling was wrong and that the Kincaids had no part in Sadie's disappearance. Rhett had been abandoned by his dad and then his mom after she succumbed to alcohol. If it turned out the sheriff was guilty, it'd be the second family Rhett lost.

Brandi averted her eyes and shuffled back, increasing the distance between them, which told Rhett his ex-fiancée was hiding something. Whether she'd found evidence or learned something about her family, he didn't know. "Do you need more time to look things over?"

"Nope. I think I'm good." She glanced around the room, her blond hair swinging over her shoulder before she took Levi from him and led him out the door.

Rhett stared after her. The room was clean. The closet door cracked open. He swung the door back and glanced inside. The denim jacket Brandi had been looking at hung on a hanger. He performed a quick search of the pockets and found nothing. A glance at the rest of the items didn't draw his attention. For a few seconds, he stared at the stuffed bear on the bed.

He could only imagine the pain of losing a child or a sister of that age. If Pam had disappeared, he would've driven himself mad trying to find her. He had thought he'd been patient with Brandi during the initial investigation, trying to help her while not stepping on his uncle's toes. But then Brandi had broken off the engagement and his tolerance had flown out the window.

He strode to the living room and found Brandi sitting on the hearth, her head down and her hands folded in her lap. Levi played at her feet with his truck and made *vroom-vroom* noises. Was she praying? Rhett suddenly felt like he was intruding. Maybe he should've been talking with the Lord, too. He shoved his hands into his pockets and stared at his feet. *Please, God, be with Brandi. Don't let her feel alone but be with her. Amen.*

When he glanced up, Brandi was staring at him. He cleared his throat. "Is there anything else you need to check out?"

"No." With her eyebrows furrowed, she shook her head. "I can't imagine anything of value would be in the attic."

"What about the garage?" Normally, Rhett wouldn't go into someone's home without a warrant, but he'd been prepared not to take any documents if he found them. Neither he nor Brandi had removed anything.

Outside, darkness had descended. "I think it's time we go."

She glanced on the clock on the wall and climbed to her feet. "I didn't realize it was so late. I guess most medical clinics are closed at this hour."

"Does your head hurt?" Concern shook him. "Are you feeling lightheaded? Get in the truck. I'm taking you to the ER."

"No. No. No. Nothing like that." Her laugh stopped and her smile wavered as she stared at the wall for several long seconds.

He moved in front of her and laid his hand on her shoulder. "What is it?"

"I was just thinking out loud." She wet her lips and dug a slip of paper out of her back pocket. "I found this in Sadie's denim jacket."

And Brandi was debating whether she should tell him? He had hoped they were making progress. He took the note and read it. "Let me guess. This is the address to a clinic."

"Yeah." She nodded. "I figure it was the place that

confirmed Sadie's pregnancy. The timeline works if Levi is the age we think he is."

"Or she could've had a cold." At Brandi's glare, he held his hands and chuckled. "Let me check the clinic's hours. If they're open, we can run by."

He pulled out his cell phone and typed in the address while Brandi looked over his shoulder, the clean smell of her shampoo wafting to him. The fragrance eluded him, but it was the same scent she'd used while they were dating. What was he looking at? Oh, yeah. The clinic's hours. "Eight to six Monday through Friday. They won't be open until Monday."

She sighed. "I figured that. Probably couldn't have told us anything because of the privacy laws."

"I agree. They couldn't tell us if Sadie were a patient and couldn't confirm who is Levi's father."

"Right."

He scooped up Levi into his arms. "Are you ready to go?"

"Yeah. But I don't have any extra clothes with me. Let me grab some of mine from my closet." At his nod, she hurried to her old room and dug out a few of her winter clothes she could still wear and stuffed them into an old backpack she found on the top shelf. "Got 'em."

As he waited for her so he could lock the door, he noticed she appeared a thousand miles away. "What is it?"

Brandi walked out the door, a chilly breeze whipping her hair. "I'd like to go back to the farm."

"Tonight?" No way.

"Since Sadie called me, maybe she left a message on Grandma's answering machine."

"Come on. Let's get Levi out of the cold." He put the boy in the truck and turned the heat on high. It had been so long since Rhett had used anything but a cell, he forgot some older people had never made the switch. "She had a landline?"

"Sure. I don't know if Grandma had it disconnected."

"The answering machine would still have the messages. How recent the messages are would depend on when the phone service was disconnected. Have you tried to call your grandmother's number?"

"No. I'm not thinking clearly. Of course, I should've called. Give me a second." She punched in the number and hit Speaker.

The machine said, "Leave a name and a number."

Brandi smiled and hung up. "Grandma was no-nonsense and claimed technology was for the young. Did the police check her messages?"

"I don't know. They could have before or after I was there. I was distracted when I spotted you at the shed."

"I don't need the reminder." Her blue eyes connected with his. "Can we go check it out?"

He rolled his head, trying to relax his stiff neck muscles. "I think we should wait until morning."

"Morning?" She sighed. "We'll be noticeable in the daylight. The electricity is still on. All I want to do is make certain Sadie didn't leave Grandma a message. It's dark, but it's not late. Maybe Sadie didn't know Grandma had moved into an assisted-living facility and said her goodbyes on the machine or mentioned her plans."

He didn't like the idea of them stopping by the farm. He was used to working with other law officers, not his ex-fiancée, even though she had been trained at the police academy, by him.

"Okay. We'll stop long enough to listen to the answering machine and then we leave." He arched his eyebrows in warning. "Deal?"

She saluted him, sarcasm her go-to defense. "Yes sir, Ranger, sir. What could go wrong?"

He ignored her gibe. Even though she sounded confident, he knew Brandi was scared for Sadie's safety, or he would never consider going to the farm.

The note she'd found in Sadie's jacket came to his mind. Brandi better not be hiding anything else.

SEVEN

Okay, there was no need to push Rhett's buttons. He'd agreed to take her. She had been on her own and didn't enjoy having to work with anyone. The good thing about being independent was you did what you thought was best, with no discussion.

She thought he was through talking, but then he said, "I'm on your side, Brandi. You can talk to me about anything."

Was he fishing for information? Moonlight filtered through the trees, casting eerie beams of light into the cab of the truck. She continued to stare out of the windshield. What could she say that wouldn't come out wrong? She knew Rhett was trying, but if you leaned on others, it gave them an opportunity to hurt you. She was better off depending on no one.

You can talk to me about anything.

About what?

He watched her. She could feel it, and since it would be awkward to let the silence go on, she turned to him. "I know you're trying to help."

He glanced her way, but evidently, by the way he hurried to get his eyes back on the road, he noticed she didn't confirm he was on her team.

Guilt washed over her. He wanted what she couldn't give. She would never trust him or anyone else.

The note and the ring came back to her mind. The clinic's address didn't surprise her because Sadie would want to confirm her pregnancy, and the time frame fit. But Brandi had assumed Sadie had met someone after she left Mulberry Gap. The ring didn't prove Wes Kincaid was the father, but it brought him to the front of the daddy list.

If Wes had still been involved with her little sister, why hadn't anyone mentioned it during the investigation?

"Don't forget. We're not staying long." Rhett's voice snapped her attention back to him.

"As if you have to remind me."

She turned toward Levi to avoid Rhett's scrutiny. Her ex had always been good at reading her mind. "I can't believe you're still awake."

Levi kicked his feet and yelled something incomprehensible.

Brandi laughed. "You're such a happy little guy."

Levi's dark eyes shined back at her. Brandi tried to see if she could see Wes in him, but Sadie also had dark eyes and hair. As did a couple of the other guys Sadie been seeing at the time of her disappearance.

Maybe that was a problem. The daddy didn't know he was a father. She really wished Sadie had confided in her.

Brandi was ready to get this over with and head home for the night. Or back to Rhett's place since she had Levi to protect. Sleep would hopefully clear her mind. Rhett parked with his headlights shining on the three-story house. The constant family get-togethers were gone forever. Her grandparents would never live here again. Her grandmother would never serve the turkey at Thanksgiving, and Dad would never say a blessing for the food.

There was nothing more Brandi would love than for her and Sadie to scrub and clean the massive house when all this was over. They wouldn't be able to repair everything, like where the roof leaked by the fireplace, but hopefully they could spend an afternoon rifling through the old keepsakes. Brandi could take her grandmother to visit the house for the weekend. Mom would probably be too busy with Phil to come, but that was fine.

Actually, it wasn't fine, but Brandi couldn't worry about the things she couldn't control.

"Are you okay?"

She jumped at the intrusion.

"You look a million miles away."

"Of course." She plastered on a smile she was certain came off as fake. "Let's listen to the answering machine and get out of here."

Rhett paused a second before getting out of the truck. About the time she opened the door and saw him standing there, she realized he'd meant to assist her. She smiled. "I got it."

"I can see that."

He'd always opened the door for her when they were dating. Some of her friends thought the gesture archaic, but Brandi had respected it. She got Levi out of his car seat, and they walked up the wooden walk to the back porch. Rhett opened the door. "Did you leave this unlocked?"

She shook her head. "I wasn't the last one here—the investigators were. The key was lost years ago. Grandma grew up in a time when no one locked their doors, even at night."

"I get it. People left the windows wide open, so why lock the doors?"

"Right." She stepped in and her gaze dropped to the mud on the linoleum floor. "The investigators could've wiped their feet."

"They should've worn protective covers over their shoes," Rhett grumbled. He bent over and ran his finger though the mud. "This is wet."

"Like it's fresh?"

He nodded. "No one should've been in here the last few hours. I'll put a lock on all the exterior doors so people can't come and go."

"I agree." There'd never been a need before, and it troubled Brandi to think how many things had changed. Knowing the gunman had run through the house made her feel violated. Funny, she'd always heard victims use that phrase, but it hadn't hit home until now.

"Where's the phone? Wait…" He crossed the room. "Here it is."

The old rectangular answering machine was one of the first models. "It has been sitting here for almost a year. I'll be surprised if the device is not full of sales calls."

"I agree," he said. "It's a long shot."

"Doesn't look like the investigators checked it out." She rewound the tape before hitting the dust-covered play button.

"Mom. It's me." Her dad's voice.

Brandi's knees wobbled and almost gave way, and she grabbed the corner of the shelf for support. "Something has come up. I won't be able to cut up those limbs today. I'll check on you later. Love you."

Her dad's voice sounded strained. She exchanged glances with Rhett. "Was this the day Dad died? Why did Grandma fail to erase the message?"

"The date and time aren't displayed. Your dad could've left the message weeks or even months before his death." Sympathy shone in Rhett's eyes.

"I guess so." Brandi didn't need compassion when she was doing everything in her power not to cry. Her intuition shouted no, her dad couldn't have left the message a long time before his death, because of the stress in his voice. That must've been the day he died, which was probably why Grandma had kept it. The next message was from Aunt Myra sending her condolences. Brandi's chest tightened as all the heartbreaking memories came flooding back. It took everything in her might not to show outward emotion. Suddenly, anger bubbled up again at Rhett. She had needed him. He'd been supportive at first, but then...

As if he sensed her thoughts, he reached out to touch her hand, but she withdrew and repositioned Levi on her hip, keeping her hands occupied. She could feel Rhett's eyes on her but ignored him. *Not now.*

The next three messages were from friends with words of encouragement.

"Grandma?" A pause. "It's me, Sadie. Please answer the phone. I've tried to call you several times. I need..." Her voice dropped to a whisper. "I need help."

Rhett's gaze connected with hers, but neither verbally responded.

What was the timeline? Was this before Sadie disappeared? Or after?

The next call was Phil Sandford. He only left his name and number and asked that she return his call. Brandi felt her jaws clench at the sound of the traitorous man. How long was this after her father's death? Did he already have his sights on her mom?

The next several calls were from a variety of sales-people and businesses.

Brandi was a little surprised there weren't any messages from her, but then she thought back and couldn't remember her grandmother never answering the phone.

"Grandma? It's me again, Sadie. I need to talk to you. I don't have a good number for you to call, so you must answer. Do you understand? I need you to answer the phone."

Rhett hit the pause button. "That could be after Sadie disappeared."

"Had to be, because if not, she would've left her cell number." Why did she call their grandmother but not her? Because of their fight. Sadie couldn't trust Brandi with her problems. Her chest tightened.

He nodded.

"Play the rest." Brandi was ready to hear more.

Clink. A noise sounded from outside.

They looked at each other.

"What was that?" she whispered.

He lifted his fingers to his lips. Then he mouthed, "I'll be right back."

She mouthed back, "Be careful."

Rhett turned off the lights, drowning the room into blackness. Because of the wraparound porches, little moonlight made it through the windows. The wooden floor creaked with his footsteps as he walked to the back door and stared out the glass panes. He continued to walk the perimeter of the lower floor.

He returned and whispered. "It was probably only the

wind, but I'm going to check outside to be certain. Stay here with Levi."

She would've argued, but he walked out the door, not giving her the chance.

"'Ett." Levi's big brown eyes stared toward the door.

"Rhett will be right back." As Brandi's eyes adjusted to the lights being out, she pulled the toddler closer and bounced him slightly on her hip to keep him quiet.

The Victorian home was beautiful when filled with laughter and family, but not so much when you were alone in the dark. Now all she heard was the wind blowing through the windowpanes and through the upstairs rooms. How did Grandma stay by herself at night? Brandi shook off the chill.

Something scurried in the next room.

Brandi's heart leaped into her throat, and she hurried to the back door. She inched it open and peered out. Rhett's truck sat in the drive with its headlights blinding her. Where was Rhett?

She stepped out on the back porch and rubbed her arms against the cold. Should they make a run for the truck?

Rhett didn't see anyone, but footprints lay scattered underneath the dining room window. Whether the impressions had been left tonight or earlier in the day, he didn't know, but anyone looking through that window had an excellent view of the living room where he and Brandi were just standing.

With his gun drawn, he continued to check out the perimeter. He didn't see anyone.

Something felt off. Like someone was there. Watching him.

The wind blew, causing the branches of a Texas sage to brush against the side of the house. Dark shadows of an outbuilding, a grain silo and old farm equipment standing in dead grass dotted the horizon. The large barn towered in the distance, casting an enormous silhouette. A door or window creaked in the building.

His eyes adjusted to the lack of light as he continued to stare at the barn. Tightening his grip on the Glock, he quietly headed that way.

He'd only taken a couple of steps when Brandi plowed into the back of him.

"I told you to stay put."

She clasped her chest. "You scared me half to death. I'm not staying in the house alone. I was going to get in the truck, but then I saw you and wanted you to know I wasn't in the house."

"I'm looking for an intruder, and you could've gotten yourself killed."

"Don't be so dramatic."

The words probably came more from fear than any intended criticism. He held up his gun and shook it.

"Sorry. I guess you're right," she conceded. "Not smart to startle an armed man. Did you see anyone?"

"No, but there're footprints under the window, so somebody's been looking inside."

"Oh, don't tell me that."

He glanced back at the barn. Only the normal movement of grass and branches from a large hackberry tree scraping against the back side of the structure. The rundown cattle lot blocked his view of the north side, and he couldn't be certain if anyone were there.

"What? What are you looking at?" She gazed in the same direction as he was. "Is something out there?"

"I don't know." Someone could've easily parked on the other side of the barn and stayed out of sight. "Let's finish up here and then get out."

She turned to go back inside when something caught his eye. He grabbed the back of her shirt. "What?"

He nodded, indicating something by the barn.

"Is that a vehicle?" She squinted.

"Looks like it. I didn't see a vehicle earlier today except for the deputies'."

Brandi shook her head. "Grandma didn't have anything parked there."

He was tempted to drive around the pasture to the back of the barn to see if anyone were watching them, but he couldn't chance it with Brandi and Levi. He wouldn't put them in the crossfire.

He said, "Come on. Let's go. It's too cold out here, anyway."

"Aren't you going to find out who that is? It might be Sadie."

"Not with you and Levi. It might be one of the gunmen. I'd need backup."

"Then call your Ranger friend—whatever his name is."

"Luke Dryden." He'd already informed Luke of the situation, but since the Texas Rangers weren't officially on the case, he hated to ask for assistance. "I will contact him later."

Rhett didn't enjoy arguing with her. There might be two or more men in the vehicle, and he had no idea how many weapons. Even with Luke, it might be too much. If he didn't have Brandi and Levi to protect, he'd do it. He finally added, "Too risky."

She frowned. "What if it's Sadie?"

"Then she should recognize you and shouldn't be hiding in the shadows and peering in windows." He headed for his truck and was relieved when she followed. They got in, buckled Levi, and he drove through the pasture toward the front entrance instead of using the drive that would take them within a few yards of the barn. A constant look into his mirror showed the hidden vehicle hadn't moved.

As soon as they were within a hundred yards of the entrance, she said, "Do something."

He drew in a deep breath and slowed his truck. "Would you like me to call the sheriff's department?"

"No," she replied before the question was all the way out. "Couldn't we sit across from the pasture? We'd have time to get away or call the sheriff if needed."

"Didn't work earlier today when you tried it. And we still don't know who attacked you. We're doing this the safe way."

"I only want to find Sadie. She left Levi in Grandpa's truck. Maybe she's in there now, waiting for me. Turn off your lights and drive around the pasture the long way, out of sight, and see who's out there."

The desperation in her voice tugged at his heart, but he still wouldn't take the chance. He'd considered the same thing. "I'm sor—"

Bright lights suddenly shot through the driver's side window, blinding him. They should've left sooner.

"Watch out," she screamed.

He glanced away from the glare and gassed his truck. They bounced across the rough terrain. The other truck, a large dually, traveled across the pasture with mud kicking up and stood between Rhett and the gate, blocking an escape.

The vehicle's lights came on by the barn and sped their way. The beams were low, like that of a car.

"There's two of them."

The dually turned toward them, the lights growing brighter through his windshield. Rhett squinted. He recognized that truck.

His heart constricted as the vehicle swished in front of them, blocking their path. He tensed, prepared in case it rammed them, but the tires skidded to a stop just in time.

"Go," Brandi yelled.

Rhett shook his head and held up his hand. "No. It'll be okay."

His uncle got out of the dually and strode to his window.

Rhett rolled it down. "Uncle Duke. What's going on?" He couldn't keep the anger from his voice.

"Don't you think I should ask you the same thing?"

Wes pulled up in his red sports car to this side of his dad's truck. Careless kid would probably ruin a tire in this pasture.

"We came to check on something in Brandi's grandma's house." Rhett purposely didn't specify they came to listen to the phone messages. "Were you and Wes looking for something?"

Even in the poor lighting, the flush of the sheriff's face burned clear. "This is a crime scene. Neither of you should be here. Especially at night. It's a good way to get yourself shot."

Rhett stared at the man who'd always been his hero. Neither he nor Wes should be at the farm. What were they doing in the barn? Looking for evidence? Or planting it?

Even though Rhett didn't intend to prod the sheriff, he was also a Texas lawman and had sworn to do his duty.

Wes came up beside his dad. "What were y'all doing here?"

Rhett noticed the twinge of nervousness in his cousin's voice. Wes might be the easy way to extract information. Instead of answering the question, Rhett smiled. "What were you doing looking in the house?"

"Wh-what?" The twenty-one-year-old blew up. "I don't owe you an explanation, cousin." The last word held sarcasm.

His uncle's voice lowered and took on a serious tone. His eyes locked with Rhett's. "You have no idea what you're getting yourself into, boy."

Was that a warning?

Brandi leaned forward. "Actually, this is my grandmother's place. I'd like to know why you're here."

The sheriff cleared his throat. "It's an ongoing investigation. We have a right to be here, Miss Callahan. In case you've forgotten, somebody shot one of my deputies this morning."

His uncle was stalling, and Rhett knew it. Rhett also realized the sheriff would never explain his reasons. He and Brandi would be better off checking the barn tomorrow to see if they could figure out what his uncle and cousin had been doing. "We understand, Uncle. Have you learned anything more on the case?"

The sheriff's eyes narrowed. "It's an ongoing investigation. I'm not at liberty to say."

Rhett nodded. "We'll see you later, then." He didn't want to give the sheriff time to turn his attention to Brandi. He put the truck into Drive and circled around the dually and to the gate before they could ask more questions.

"Why did you do that? Why let them off the hook?"

Rhett rolled up his window and exited the pasture to the road. He turned right toward the shed. "Even if they were up to no good, they would never admit it. We don't need to get on the sheriff's bad side."

"It's probably too late for that," she spouted. She stared out the window. "Your uncle scares me."

Rhett didn't blame her for feeling that way. He had never been on the opposite side of the sheriff before and didn't want to go there. Brandi had never trusted the man, and that had always bugged Rhett. He'd always believed she would come to respect his uncle as soon as she got to know him better.

Maybe Rhett was the one who would come to change his opinion of the man.

You have no idea what you're getting yourself into, boy. The threat kept going off in his head. What had his uncle meant?

She turned toward him. "Did Wes seem nervous to you?"

"Yes." Rhett released a breath. He didn't know if she'd heard his uncle's words, but he didn't intend to repeat them now. "My cousin has always had a chip on his shoulder. As a teen, he got in trouble repeatedly and his dad bailed him out."

"I remember. He was a year older than Sadie, but she always liked him."

Rhett glanced her way. "What are you saying?"

"Nothing. I just don't trust them. This situation is off."

Almost exactly his earlier thoughts. He went past the shed and kept going until he came to the next small drive. There was no culvert, but the farmer used the entrance to bring their tractors into the field. He cut his lights and turned into the drive.

"Can I assume you're watching to see what they do?"

He nodded. "I didn't see their vehicles pull out, but I want to know when they leave."

"Good. Me, too."

The distance was over a half a mile to the barn, but he could see the glow of the headlights. They weren't trying to hide this time.

"What do you suppose they're doing?" She leaned forward and grabbed the dash.

"I don't know." But he didn't like the ideas that kept running through his mind.

"I think they're either removing evidence or planting it."

Almost exactly his previous thought. "Or maybe the sheriff got to thinking about a piece of evidence he'd forgotten and decided to check it out."

"In his personal truck? And why bring Wes along?"

That bugged Rhett, as well. He couldn't think of a reason. Wes worked at the detention center, not in investigations. There was no reason for him to be there.

"Wes and Sadie dated for a while."

"I know." Rhett had learned that after he explored Sadie's disappearance. "They quit dating months before Sadie vanished. Wes had been a troubled teen but has his act together now."

"Are you kidding me? I know you love your family, but surely you can be objective. It looks fishy them being out here at night when no one else is around. Why did they keep their lights off like they were trying to keep their presence a secret?"

"I don't know." He didn't like the implications, either. "They could've been observing the house to see if anyone showed up. It could've been anyone milling around your grandmother's house."

"There they go." Brandi pointed across the pasture.

Sure enough, two sets of headlights went across the field and turned onto the road going in the opposite direction. Rhett waited a couple of minutes before he backed out of the drive and turned to the right.

"Where are you going? Don't you want to go check it out? See if they planted anything. Mainly to incriminate me?"

He kept going away from the farm. "Not tonight. I'm going to get you to safety. If anything new shows up in the morning, we'll know they planted it."

"Come on. That's ridiculous and you know it. If the sheriff's department 'finds' something in the morning, they'll bag it as evidence."

He sighed. She was right, of course, but it was important to get them somewhere secure. "Your and Levi's safety is more important. I took a chance taking you here to listen to your grandmother's answering machine. I don't want to go back tonight."

EIGHT

"Where are you taking us?" Brandi looked over at Rhett. Concern was etched on his face. "Back to Mom's place?" They had grabbed burgers and fries at a drive-thru on the outskirts of Mulberry Gap, and besides the kid's burger she'd given Levi, the food remained in the bag. After today, there was no way she wanted to stay alone at her mom's place or even her own place. Too much danger.

He shook his head. "No. I want a place I can defend you better. I know a few places but they're several hours from here."

Her stomach rolled. "I don't want to leave the area in case we learn something about Sadie." She hoped he wasn't talking about his place. His house sat on a dead-end street and they would have difficulty escaping if it turned out to be necessary.

"Back to my place."

The air whooshed out of her lungs. "Won't we be trapped if someone comes looking for us since it's on a dead-end road?"

He shook his head. "I can't think of a better place. There's only one approach, and I have a side-by-side all-terrain vehicle in the shed. If we must leave, we can take it on the trails until we reach McLean Lane."

"You have a Rhino? I didn't know that." The four-wheeled sport vehicle was roomier and more stable than most ATVs. It might not be as comfortable as the truck, but all three of them could ride in it if necessary.

"Yeah, I bought it last year from a friend whose wife made him get rid of it." Rhett smiled—something he should try more often. "Evidently, the guy didn't discuss the purchase with her before time."

"I can see where that would be a problem. Okay. I suppose your place it is. I'm starving."

"Me, too." He glanced in his rearview mirror. "Looks like the little man is out."

A glance over her shoulder showed Levi's head had fallen to his shoulder. To be able to fall asleep so easily would be wonderful.

Light pings hit the hood of the truck.

"Is it raining?"

He said, "No. That's sleet."

"Great."

Darkness had fallen. Brandi should be sleepy since she'd been awake over thirty-six hours, but she couldn't stop her thoughts long enough to relax. The wipers beat in rhythm and the headlights reflected off the steadily falling sleet. The temperatures had been cold long enough; the moisture would stick. She glanced at the speedometer and noticed Rhett had slowed his speed considerably. Not many people were out on the roads. "Is it slick?"

"Not yet. But if this continues, it will be in another hour."

Maybe that would make it more difficult for someone to follow them. It was uncommon for north Texas to receive measurable frozen precipitation and the counties didn't clear the roads if they became icy. Most people took a snow day and stayed home until it melted—normally only a day or two.

She looked at him. "You think the Bronco would have any difficulty making it out to your place?"

He sighed. "I doubt it. It'd have to get a lot worse, and I don't think the forecast is calling for snow. But sleet wasn't in the forecast, either."

Brandi had thought the same thing. She glanced down at her phone and checked for messages or missed calls. There were none. She prayed Sadie wasn't exposed to this weather but had a dry warm place to stay the night. Why didn't her sister simply call?

If Brandi had Sadie's number, it was the first thing she'd do. And if Sadie didn't know whether Brandi had the same number, she should know Brandi still worked in dispatch. Sadie could get ahold of Shannon. Her sister had always been street-smart. Where there was a will, there was a way. Right?

Which brought up the same question that had been going round and round in her mind ever since she found Levi in the truck. Why hadn't Sadie come for her son?

Because she couldn't. Not because Sadie didn't care for Levi. No one could turn their back on that sweet little boy.

Brandi clung to her seat belt strap like her life depended on it. What would happen to Levi if Sadie weren't found or was discovered dead? The thought was too despairing. Her sister was safe somewhere waiting for Brandi to find her. *Please, God, let Sadie be alive for the little boy's sake.*

She had never said a more sincere prayer.

Rhett turned the truck off the pavement and onto the rock road. Brandi stared out the window. Everything appeared so desolate with the ground turning white. The wide-open pastures were separated by barbwire fences. Only a spattering of trees could be seen in the distance. A small herd of cattle hunkered down in a small valley. The sleet had collected in the ditches and lightly covered the road. No tracks could be seen.

He drove through the entrance to his place and then stopped. "I'll lock my gate tonight."

Rhett got out and secured a heavy-duty chain to the metal gate. She waited while he jogged back to the truck. He shook the chill from him, and cold air whisked into the cab.

The long driveway ended at his small home.

"Let me go in and check things out."

While he was gone, she looked around at their surroundings. No other houses were in sight, but a lone security light from his closest neighbor glowed in the misty night.

Rhett returned a couple of minutes later. "All clear. I turned the heat up. It shouldn't take long to warm the house." He grabbed their few bags of supplies and the backpack while she got Levi out of the truck. The little fellow whined and laid his head on her shoulder.

The cold wind blasted her, and she hurried to the front door, careful not to fall on the slippery steps. Rhett came in behind her with his arms full.

Warm air hit her, and she moved to the couch to lay Levi down.

Rhett dropped the diaper bag on the floor and put the bag with burgers on the table. "You and Levi can stay in my room. If you want to get him dressed for bed, I'll get us something to drink."

"You don't have to give up your room. We can stay in the guest room."

"Nonsense. I only have a cot in there, and I'd rather stay on the couch. There's a pack of new toothbrushes in the bottom drawer in the bathroom cabinet."

Rhett wasn't fooling her. He didn't plan to sleep tonight. And if he were on the couch, an attacker would have to go through him to get to her. She kept the thought to herself and did as he asked. She appreciated his thoughtfulness.

Sleet pelted the two windows, sending a shiver up her spine. "Sounds like it's picking up."

He glanced out the window. "Yeah, it's really coming down now."

Levi stirred on the couch. "I'll be right back." She grabbed his diaper bag and went to the bedroom to change his diaper and clothes.

Levi rolled over and closed his eyes as soon as she laid him on the bed. "Hold on. Let's get you into something more comfortable."

Rhett called from the other room, "I'm going to get a fire going."

"Okay." She quickly changed Levi and piled pillows around him to prevent him from falling off the bed. She waited to make sure he was asleep before she stepped out of the room, leaving the door cracked open.

Rhett had a fire going in the fireplace and the smell of fries filled the room. Despite every muscle in her body screaming from lack of energy, starvation won. "Smells good."

"I reheated the burgers in the microwave and tossed the fries into the fryer long enough to get them warm."

She found paper plates in the pantry and set them on the table. Even though the fire was blazing, the room still held a chill. She paused. "Do you mind if we eat in front of the fireplace?"

"That'd be perfect. Shouldn't admit this, but I eat on the couch often."

"Me, too." She smiled as she moved the food into the living room. That was something she and Rhett had in common. Living by herself, she found it unnecessary to sit at the table. Vegging in front of the television made her meals not so lonely.

Rhett brought a couple of Cokes to the coffee table. "Coke Zero?"

"You remembered."

"Your favorite." He thrust it into the air in toast-like fashion.

And he preferred peach tea if it was available. Just like her daddy.

Brandi took the seat closet to the fire, but as Rhett settled in the older chair beside her, he bowed his head. She joined him as he gave thanks for the food.

Mild awkwardness settled in the quiet. She squirted a hefty dose of ketchup on the fries, salted them and popped one in her mouth.

It'd been a long time since she'd spent time with Rhett. Him saying the blessing at every meal had always impressed her. He not only went to worship services but practiced his faith in everyday life, no matter the circumstances. She hated to admit, she tended to get sidetracked when life got stressful. At work, she had to catch a bite here and there. Her lunch break often got cut short and she'd forget to tell God thanks for the food. She was glad Rhett had kept his faith.

She finally broke the silence. "What are we going to do?"

He glanced at her. "I'm not certain until we learn who's after you."

"For tonight, I don't mind staying here. I need to get my thoughts together. But I need to find Sadie."

"Brandi..."

She shook her head. "Don't do this, Rhett. You know I must find her. She reached out to me."

"Did she?"

She narrowed her eyes. "What are you trying to say?"

"Why call 911 if she was trying to reach you? You haven't changed numbers, and I'm certain she didn't forget it."

Irritation crawled all over her and she placed her untouched burger on the coffee table.

"Don't do that." He cocked his head. "Don't get mad."

"I'm not mad." Upset, but not mad.

"You got to admit it's a good question. And if it was Sadie who called, why didn't she wait on you?"

That question had been swirling around her mind ever since early this morning. "You heard the call. It was disconnected. Don't you think she got interrupted?"

"Could have. Or maybe she wanted you to take Levi."

"But why? I can't imagine anyone who'd attack a toddler." Brandi could tell by his expression he was thinking the situation over. Nothing made sense. And Rhett hadn't mentioned it, for which she was glad, but Sadie had started dabbling in marijuana before she disappeared. Was it possible she had started doing even stronger drugs? Levi didn't seem to have any signs of drug exposure.

Rhett handed her burger back to her. "Eat. Please."

She took it. Even as he made the gesture, she noticed he'd barely touched his plate.

Quietly, she ate her burger and fries. When the last bite was gone, she realized she couldn't remember eating it. "Thank you."

"Would you like something else?"

"No."

He took her plate along with his half-eaten burger and tossed them in the trash. When he returned, she noticed the lines under his eyes showing fatigue. His expression was serious. Back when they'd dated, he'd been carefree and fun. There were a few serious times, but Rhett always bounced back full of energy. He was one of those people whose smile lit up the room; everyone wanted to be his friend. Sometimes people mistook his cheer to believe he didn't carry heavy burdens, but Brandi knew better.

Once after working a case where the family had neglected a child, Rhett had been so fraught with anger, it shocked her. She had never seen him that down. It was then that he confided in her about the day his dad had left. She could still recall his hands shaking with emotion as he described how he'd sprinted out of his house to catch his dad.

Rhett never recited the exact words, but she knew he had begged his dad to stay. Before he could finish telling the story, Rhett's voice had broken.

She always speculated what his dad had said to him that day.

As she stared at him, she wondered what emotions were built up inside of him. His uncle Duke had taken him and his sister in and Rhett would always be grateful. Her mind went back to the look on his uncle's face tonight as he walked up to Rhett's truck.

There was something about the sheriff she didn't trust.

"What are you thinking?"

Rhett's interruption caught her off guard. "Wondering why your uncle and cousin were at the farm tonight."

Rhett ran his fingers through his hair and sat on the couch, but not too close. She noticed he kept his distance, which she appreciated. It was not that she didn't wish well for her ex-fiancé, because she did. Rhett seemed to understand and respect her wishes. There was no way she could work with him if he sought to renew their relationship.

"That has been on my mind, as well."

"I know you're close to your uncle and aunt, but just keep an open mind while we're looking for Sadie."

His eyes held hers. "You don't have to remind me. I understand the ramifications. Remember, I deal with facts."

Maybe Rhett thought he did, but Brandi could tell him from experience that there was nothing worse than betrayal from the ones you loved. She decided against voicing her concern, for it would do no good unless they found evidence that proved her fears.

A log settled and the crackling of falling embers filled the silence. If it weren't for the situation, it could've been a serene setting. The pings of sleet hitting the house had subsided.

The lull began to take over her mind, making her feel a sudden awareness of them being alone. Their last Christmas together, they'd sat in front of a fire after exchanging gifts. She and Rhett had stayed up late drinking hot chocolate and watching Christmas movies until after midnight.

Life had been full of hope then, fun and bursting with dreams. Looking back, she realized she'd been a naive girl believing life would be rainbows and lollipops. Well, maybe not that dreamy, but at least she believed Rhett and she would both have a career in law enforcement and her family would be a big part of their life.

Was he thinking along the same lines? Glad he'd gotten to know her better before they had committed their life together in matrimony? Or had he moved on, doing his duty by keeping her safe? The thought that she meant nothing to him bothered her a little.

She stood. "I'm going to turn in for the night."

"That's a good idea. It's been a long day and you need your sleep. How's your head?" He got to his feet and reached up. Gingerly, he touched where the board had hit her.

"Better. Just a slight headache." She pulled away enough to break the contact. "Working the night shift makes it easy to mix up my days and nights, but I'm dragging right now and can't think anymore."

He sent her a sympathetic look before withdrawing his gun from a drawer in the coffee table. "I'm going to check the perimeter before we settle in."

"Okay." She preferred the distance between them. After he shrugged into his coat and walked out the back door, she went into the bedroom and closed the door. Quietly, so as to not wake Levi, she grabbed the backpack and carried it to the bed. She found an old pair of sweatpants and a T-shirt and changed. Normally, the thick pants would be too bulky to sleep in, but she wanted to be prepared in case they needed to leave in a hurry.

After brushing her teeth, she heard the door open and shut, then the lock clicked. A shuffling said Rhett was back on the couch. To make certain she could hear if anyone tried to break in, she cracked her bedroom door open.

Rhett glanced up at her. His Glock lay on the coffee table and he held his laptop across his legs.

"Good night," she whispered.

"Night, Brandi."

Their eyes held for just a moment before she pulled away and crawled into bed. She stared up at the ceiling and listened to Levi's soft breathing and the occasional popping of a log in the fireplace.

Two years of avoiding Rhett, and here she was: in less than twenty-fours of seeing him, he'd stepped back into the role of protector.

It was not so much that she minded his help as that she'd run straight to him. Why had she done that? No one else had even crossed her mind. She could've run to Shannon or one of her other coworkers. Surely Rhett wouldn't get the wrong idea and think she wanted to rekindle their relationship? If he did, it would be her own fault.

Moonlight shone through the slats of the blinds, and only occasionally sleet dinged the window.

Where was Sadie? If another dispatcher had answered the emergency call or if Brandi had missed the meaning of the farm, what would've been Levi's fate?

Her sister was in danger, but would Brandi be able to stay alive long enough to help her? A clicking of the keyboard sounded from the living room as her eyes drifted closed. She was grateful Rhett was keeping watch over them.

NINE

The next morning, the sun shone bright, but the temperatures remained below freezing. Rhett had finally convinced Brandi they should go to his sister's house so she could help with Levi. After last night, he didn't cotton to the idea of the toddler being with him and Brandi as they followed clues. He wanted to protect them, but he also needed to find out what who was behind the attacks. Pam, his sister, took self-defense classes and was quite good with a gun. Rhett didn't think anyone would look for Brandi at his sister's house, but if they did, they would be in for a surprise since both women were capable.

Last night after Brandi went to bed, he'd talked to Luke Dryden to keep him abreast of the situation. His fellow Ranger had let him know there was no change in Deputy Norris's condition, and he had turned Phil's bank withdrawal receipt over to Chasity Spears at the Texas Rangers headquarters in Austin. If information could be found, Chasity would find it.

"Are you sure Pam doesn't mind helping us? I can stay at a hotel in town." Forehead wrinkled, Brandi stared at the floorboard of his truck as they drove to Pam's.

She had always hated to ask for assistance and was even worse now.

"Not at all. Too many people coming and going at a hotel to know which ones could be a suspect and who is a legitimate customer. Pam said she'd be glad to help. My sister always liked you." The two had played basketball together and had run on the same mile-relay team in high school two years before Rhett and Brandi started dating.

"I know." Brandi swallowed. "It's just that things ended on such a bad note when you and I broke up. I haven't seen her since."

"Don't worry. You know Pam." He pulled into his sister's drive and put his truck into Park.

Brandi pursed her lips in thought.

"Let's go in." He chuckled. "You'll see." His sister and Brandi had gotten along great from the moment they met. Yes, Pam had been upset for a few months after Brandi broke their engagement. Then she'd finally conceded Brandi had a lot on her plate, with her dad's death and Sadie's disappearance. Rhett thought Pam's initial frustration had been disappointment that Brandi wasn't going to be her sister-in-law, and she didn't like to see Rhett upset. He hadn't given it much thought, but his sister had always treated him like her big brother hero.

He grabbed the diaper bag and suitcase while Brandi got Levi. He observed their surroundings before approaching the house. His sister's car was parked outside the garage. The next-door neighbor opened the side door and let her dog into her yard. Nothing appeared amiss, but he didn't intend on staying outside longer than necessary.

Pam's front door flew open. "Get in out of the cold." His sister stepped back to give them room to enter. Pam stood at five foot four and probably didn't weigh a hundred and ten. Her ash-blond hair was pulled back into a ponytail. With her small frame, and attired in a pair of comfy penguin sweats, she wouldn't lead anyone to guess she held a black belt in karate.

"Thank you." Brandi shook off the cold as she crossed the threshold. "I really appreciate this, Pam. I'm sorry I haven't stayed in touch."

"It's been a long time and people get busy. You're looking great." She pointed to the back of the house. "Rhett, you can put those things in the guest bedroom."

As he went down the hallway, he heard his sister begin to fuss and coo over Levi. He grinned. Pam had a soft spot for babies.

While he had a little privacy, he shut the bedroom door. He had several missed calls from his uncle, and he hit his number.

"Where are you?" his uncle bellowed.

Rhett held the phone away from his ear and swallowed down the automatic irritation at his uncle's tone. At times his uncle could be rude, but Rhett didn't let it bother him. He also realized the sheriff didn't like being left out of the loop. "I needed to get Brandi and Levi somewhere safe. Someone attacked her again yesterday afternoon, and I'm afraid we won't be able to protect her."

"What do you mean attacked her again?" His voice dropped to a normal level. "When?"

"Yesterday afternoon." Rhett didn't want to get into details because he didn't know what part, if any, his uncle had played in the incident.

"Why didn't you mention this last night at the farm?" The sheriff continued to talk in a loud voice.

"I figured you knew about it and didn't think to call. Deputy Zdeb questioned us about it."

"Zdeb. I wasn't notified but I'll check the reports," he mumbled. "Son, our department is good at keeping people safe. It's *our* job. You know that."

"Yes, sir. But I'm afraid there may be a leak." Actually, Brandi believed there was a leak, but he didn't want his uncle to blame her. Ever since Rhett chose to join the Texas Rangers instead of work for Jarvis County Sheriff's Department, he had to be careful not to offend his uncle by acting like the Rangers were a better agency.

"In *my* department?" the sheriff boomed.

"Not necessarily. Could be Mulberry Police Department, or no one at all. We're still gathering facts."

"The Callahans have been causing trouble for years. I know you're partial to the girl, but son, I don't think you're thinking clearly."

Rhett drew a deep breath. He'd been afraid the sheriff would make that assumption. Rhett didn't like that everyone—including his own family—blamed Brandi for her dad's crimes. *If* her dad committed a crime. Rhett needed to shift the conversation. "I've got her hidden for now. But Uncle, you know I'll do what's right. If anything leads me to believe Brandi is guilty of misconduct, I'll bring her in. You've got to trust me."

A pause on the other end of the line. "You never did say where you were keeping the girl."

The girl has a name. "No, I didn't. She's safe."

"That's not going to cut it. Where are you?"

Rhett cringed but couldn't find a way out of telling him the truth. "Pam's house."

"Good thinking. Keep her there, and we'll get to the bottom of this."

Voices traveled down the hall, and the door swung open as he hung up.

Brandi glanced at the phone and then back to him. "Sorry. Didn't mean to interrupt you."

"No problem."

She asked, "Did you learn anything?"

The concern in her eyes tugged at his heart. "Nothing yet. Have you gotten anything to eat?"

"I'm not hungry. I'm tired, but there's no way I could relax enough to sleep more than a few minutes at a time." She rubbed the back of her neck. "I want to find Sadie. I was talking with Pam, and she mentioned something I didn't know."

"What's that?"

"She said Sadie and a couple of other girls got in trouble for skipping school her junior year." Brandi stood by the bed and propped her knee on the edge. "Pam said they hid out all day at Parker Airfield."

"The abandoned place?"

Brandi nodded and her eyes glistened with hope. "Yeah. There are plenty of spots to hide out there."

Parker Airfield had been used during World War II and closed in the early eighties. It had been falling apart ever since. He narrowed his gaze. "You think she's hiding there?"

"Why not? It'd make sense. There's the aircraft hangar and the old barracks. Perfect place to hole up if she's injured or needs to disappear for a few days. If the guy in the Bronco isn't from around here, he wouldn't know to look there. He's probably checking hotels, family and friends."

"You might be right."

"Let's go see."

Determination lined her jaw. He shook his head. "I don't want you and Levi anywhere near there."

"Pam can watch Levi and I'll have you with me. If there's anything suspicious when we drive by, we'll simply leave. Sadie could be hurt, and it's not like we have any other leads."

"I agree, Sadie is the key to the attacks..." He sighed. He wanted to find Brandi's sister, too, but... "Let me ask Luke to meet me at the airfield and you stay here."

"The drive won't take us forty minutes, and Luke is over three hours away. If Sadie's not there, it'll be a wasted trip." She held her hands up. "And I *want* to go."

"No. We need to play this right. Let my uncle know the plans, too." Even as he said the words, he realized he didn't want to wait for Luke or inform the sheriff until he knew more. "I'll go to the airfield and see if she's been there."

"No way. I'm not waiting. I'm not going to sit here like some damsel in distress. I've been through police training. If Sadie's hurt, she can't wait, and the temperatures are dropping." Anger flashed red across her cheeks, and she cocked her head. "Are you going with me or not?"

He refrained from smiling. As much as he didn't like to admit it, if the roles were reversed and Pam was out there, nobody would stop him from finding her. "Let's see if Pam minds tending to Levi while we're gone."

"Pam already agreed to watch him while you were on the phone." She snapped her fingers as if saying *pronto*. She put her hand on his arm. "Let's go."

He pulled back, his arm sizzling from her touch. Brandi had always had that effect on him, and he was surprised it hadn't lessened with her absence from his life. "You know this is a long shot. I don't want you getting your hopes up."

"The last few years I've become a realist."

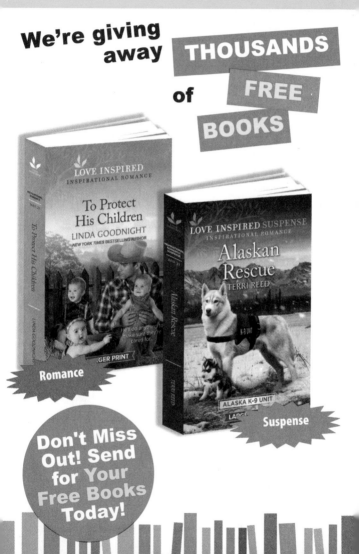

Get up to 4
FREE FABULOUS BOOKS
You Love!

To thank you for being a loyal reader we'd like to send you up to 4 FREE BOOKS, absolutely free.

Just write "YES" on the Loyal Reader Voucher and we'll send you up to 4 Free Books and Free Mystery Gifts, altogether worth over $20, as a way of saying thank you for being a loyal reader.

Try **Love Inspired® Romance Larger-Print** books and fall in love with inspirational romances that take you on an uplifting journey of faith, forgiveness and hope.

Try **Love Inspired® Suspense Larger-Print** books where courage and optimism unite in stories of faith and love in the face of danger.

Or **TRY BOTH!**

We are so glad you love the books as much as we do and can't wait to send you great new books.

So don't miss out, return your Loyal Reader Voucher Today!

Pam Powers

LOYAL READER
FREE BOOKS VOUCHER

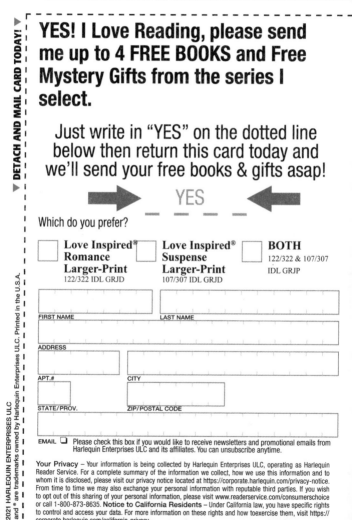

YES! I Love Reading, please send me up to 4 FREE BOOKS and Free Mystery Gifts from the series I select.

Just write in "YES" on the dotted line below then return this card today and we'll send your free books & gifts asap!

➡ YES ⬅

Which do you prefer?

| ☐ **Love Inspired®** Romance Larger-Print 122/322 IDL GRJD | ☐ **Love Inspired®** Suspense Larger-Print 107/307 IDL GRJD | ☐ **BOTH** 122/322 & 107/307 IDL GRJP |

FIRST NAME

LAST NAME

ADDRESS

APT.#

CITY

STATE/PROV.

ZIP/POSTAL CODE

EMAIL ☐ Please check this box if you would like to receive newsletters and promotional emails from Harlequin Enterprises ULC and its affiliates. You can unsubscribe anytime.

HARLEQUIN® Reader Service —Here's how it works:

As they grabbed their coats, he imagined that was true. Brandi's world had been turned upside down, her loved ones ripped from her life. He intended to see nothing else happened to her, whether she liked it or not.

Levi was in front of the television contentedly eating sliced apples and watching cartoons when Brandi told him bye. She was relieved Pam had agreed to care for him. Adrenaline flowed through Brandi's veins as she considered the airfield and the perfect hideout it made.

A few minutes later, she and Rhett were on the farm-to-market road headed northwest toward the abandoned airfield. Pam promised to put Levi down for his afternoon nap after the show was over. Hopefully, Brandi would find her sister and make it back before he woke.

The roads were almost clear of last night's sleet, but the temperatures were below freezing, and the wind strong. Occasionally, a gust hit their truck and pushed the vehicle to the right. "Is it ever going to warm up? This weather is ridiculous."

"Give it a day or two. It'll be in the seventies."

She smiled. "This year has been colder than most."

"That's true."

Once they found Sadie, they'd get to the bottom of the attacks and the emergency call. Brandi wished her sister had trusted her more with the truth. Whatever was going on in her life, Brandi could've helped.

Didn't Sadie know that?

Her mind automatically went back to the summer their dad had died. The tornadoes had hit in May, causing millions of dollars' worth of damage. Then along came June. It had been unusually hot for several consecutive days with temperatures above 100 degrees. That Thursday, her mom had arrived home late from shopping and Dad was not home. Mom couldn't reach him on his cell, and since he'd been talking about trimming trees and cutting branches left by spring storms at the farm, she'd asked Brandi to run by and remind him they were having company for dinner. When Brandi arrived, she noticed his SUV parked in the pasture between the house and the barn, but her dad was not in sight. She went into the house, figuring he had gone in for a drink or to cool off. She hadn't been alarmed when he wasn't inside. She poured her dad and herself a cola and then walked to the barn and called his name. No answer. As she entered the side room, she bumped into something.

Her dad hung from the rafters.

She'd moved so fast to get him down, she'd tripped and spilled a container of fertilizer. The liquid splashed her face, resulting in a permanent eye injury.

Brandi's chest ached, the pain radiating throughout her soul, and she shoved the vision away.

Two weeks later, Sadie had disappeared. Brandi woke that morning to learn her sister was gone. Her purse and clothes were still in her room, as if she hadn't planned to leave.

"We'll drive by first."

She jumped at Rhett's words.

"You all right?" He frowned. "You don't have to go in if you don't want to."

She smiled, embarrassed she'd been so deep in thought. "I'm not nervous. Just anxious to find Sadie."

"Me, too."

As they drew near the entrance, Rhett slowed.

Brandi leaned forward. The old airplane hangar stood against the horizon, with its curved roof and the two metal sliding doors ajar. The crumbling pavement was void of vehicles. Even though there were a few mesquite bushes, most of the area was open and bare because of the airstrip. "I don't see anyone."

"Me, neither, but I doubt somebody would park out front. Even though this road gets little traffic, a vehicle could be parked in the hangar or out back."

She agreed, and he stopped at the end of the drive behind a huge cedar tree. "What are you doing?"

He glanced at her hand, and she thought he was going to take it. Instead, he lowered his head. "Let's pray."

That was the last thing she expected him to say, but she didn't comment, and merely bowed her head.

"Please, Lord, keep us safe."

That was it? She glanced up at him to make sure he was finished and hadn't just paused. He put the truck into Drive and drove down the rock drive. Rhett had always been short and to the point.

Brandi still attended worship services and said her prayers most nights. The fact Rhett still practiced his faith didn't surprise her, but that he would pray aloud before going into a potentially dangerous situation did. She couldn't remember him being that open with his beliefs when they'd dated.

Her attention returned to the airfield. Most of the buildings had been torn down years ago. Only one of the soldiers' barracks remained and it sat north of the hangar. A door swung freely in the wind and most of the windows were broken. She drew in a deep breath, preparing her nerves. *Please, God, let Sadie be here.*

She noticed Rhett surveyed the property as they slowly made their way across the open space. He drove to the front of the hangar by the huge sliding doors the planes used to enter and exit through. From this vantage point, you could see all the way to the back of the building. Besides a few discarded, rusty tools, the place appeared forsaken.

Rhett backed up and drove around the back side of the hanger.

"Why didn't you park out front? We won't be here long. If we need to get away…"

"I don't want my truck visible from the road. We'd be spotted if the place is being watched."

Okay. That made sense.

"I'll be right back." He slid his Glock from his shoulder holster.

She wished she had brought her gun with her instead of leaving it at her house. She opened the door at the same time as he. "I'm going with you."

He frowned and stepped in front of the truck. "Stay behind me."

Trailing him closely, she followed as he passed the sliding doors. He came to a halt, and she bumped into him. "Sorry."

She observed the corners of the hangar that couldn't be seen from the truck. She let out a breath.

"I'll check out the back rooms." He strode to the far side of the building.

What appeared to be a restroom stood in the far corner. Wind blew through the open doors, causing the tin to clang and leaves to blow across the floor. Neon pink spray paint stated, "Brett was here" and "Jimena loves Ethan." Brandi paused in the middle of the floor. A piece of metal flapped against the roof, creating a loud bang that made her jump. She tugged her coat closer.

A few seconds later, Rhett returned. "Nothing. And

there's no sign anyone has been here recently." He jerked his head. "Come on. Let's check out the barracks."

She hurried to catch up to him. If Sadie were here, surely, she would've heard them pull up. Wouldn't she have spotted them and come out by now? *Not if she were hurt.* Brandi kept her doubts to herself, for she could tell Rhett was busy keeping a lookout.

As they drew closer, the barracks seemed to take on an ominous aspect. Movement in one of the windows caught her eye. A curtain dangled in the opening. Was it just the battered piece of cotton blowing in the breeze or had something else moved in that room?

"Texas Ranger Rhett Kincaid," he announced and stepped through the door.

Brandi hesitated a moment before following him inside. A musty smell assaulted her, and she gagged.

"This place gives me the creeps," she whispered after her tirade of a coughing fit.

Leaves, dirt and bits of insulation lay scattered on the floor. The wind howled through the empty rooms. Again, colorful graffiti decorated the walls, this time with disdainful words.

Rhett kept his hand on his gun, and Brandi stayed on his heels. They went to the right, to the end of the front room. A large metal door lay on the floor and the moldy odor grew almost unbearable. Bricks lined the circular walls and then plunged into darkness. "That looks like a humongous root cellar. What is it?"

Using his flashlight, he illuminated the hole. "An old air raid shelter. Considering it's full of water, it must have been caving in for a while."

Debris floated on top, and a thin layer of ice covered

the surface. "That gives me the heebie-jeebies. Sadie's definitely not in here." *Or at least she hoped.*

He jerked his head as he moved in the other direction. "Come on."

They passed several empty offices, one with a decaying desk and metal file cabinets strewn across the floor like someone had gone through leftover supplies. She listened for the sounds of movement but couldn't hear well over the wind. "It doesn't look like anyone has been here."

"I was thinking the same thing. But let's check out the building thoroughly so we can mark this place off our list of potential hiding places."

She was glad Rhett understood. At the end of the hall, banging echoed as they ascended metal stairs up to the second floor. A large open room lay before them with iron bunks, and what had once been a mattress sat in mounds of rotting fabric and padding. Her heart sank.

Sadie wasn't here.

He stole a glance at her, as if sensing her disappointment. "Let me check out the restroom."

Brandi already knew Sadie wasn't in there. But even though she understood her sister was unlikely to be here, she couldn't help getting her hopes up. Brandi simply didn't know where to look. Had Sadie dropped Levi at the farm and abandoned him for good? The thought made her sick.

Rhett returned and shook his head. "No sign of your sister. I'm sorry."

"I knew it was a long shot." She tried to smile but couldn't force it. Her heart tightened. Doubt that it was Sadie on the 911 call tugged at her. What if it wasn't her after all, and Levi belonged to someone else?

The wind whipped up the odor again. "It stinks in here."

He indicated a hole in the ceiling with a jerk of his head. "The rain has been coming in for years."

"I'm surprised the army didn't clean this out when they shut this place down." Cans of spray paint and a few syringes lay discarded on the floor. A pile of two mattresses in the corner caught her eye. That was odd. It appeared like someone had stacked them to make a comfortable bed. She continued to survey the area. Footprints in the dust and grime dotted the floor by the mattresses. "Look."

Rhett crossed the room.

"Do you see that?"

"Shoe prints." He examined the impressions. "And they appear to be recent. But it could be from a homeless person or teenagers."

Careful not to touch the prints, Brandi lined her shoe up next to the mark. "It's about the right size. I wear an eight and Sadie wore a seven and a half. We were close enough in size to share shoes." When Rhett didn't respond, she wanted to tell him Sadie had been here, but she saved her breath. She'd need more proof.

A door slammed downstairs. They both looked at each other and then Rhett ran out of the room. Brandi started to follow but faltered when her eye caught the graffiti again.

Black paint on top of a rainbow of other colors read, "I love me, too."

Brandi's throat constricted. She stared at the writing as the words penetrated.

Sadie had been here!

When they were ten and six, Brandi had hit Sadie with

a plastic bat, causing her little sister to burst into tears. Being afraid Sadie would tattle, Brandi began saying, "I'm sorry. I love you." Sadie had puckered her lip and spouted, "I love me, too." Brandi had laughed, and after that day, they began to say the phrase to one another.

Sadie had painted the message, knowing Brandi would be the only one to understand.

"Come on, Brandi," Rhett called from downstairs. "Must've been the wind."

"Okay." She glanced at the ground and took a step toward the stairs. More footprints in the dust. Her gaze followed the steps. A wooden locker sat wedged behind the bunks. Surely that was too small for someone to hide in, but maybe Sadie had left something behind. Brandi hurried over, not wanting to make Rhett wait and yanked on the door.

Bam.

The door hit her in the face and knocked her back. Pain radiated across her cheek and tears blurred her vision. A man wearing a flannel shirt sprinted from the room and down the stairs.

"Watch out, Rhett!"

TEN

Crash! The sound came from the first floor. Then a commotion erupted, with shouting and something slamming into a wall.

Brandi's body shook uncontrollably as she ran out of the room. Just as she descended the stairs, she saw Rhett standing over the man in flannel, the intruder's arm hiked behind his back.

The man squealed, "Let go. Let go. I didn't take nothin'."

After a second look, she realized the guy was more of a kid than an adult—somewhere between sixteen and eighteen.

"I'm Texas Ranger Rhett Kincaid. Identify yourself."

The kid struggled against his hold. "Brice Patterson, dude. I wasn't doin' nothing."

"Brice, when I let go, don't try to run away." Rhett's tone held authority. "I need to ask you some questions."

"Okay. Okay."

Rhett released his grip and stood. "What are you doing here?"

"Nothing." The teen slung his bangs out of his eyes and then yanked down his shirt that had ridden up.

Brandi stepped over. "Did you see a young woman here?"

Brice frowned and hesitated. "Why are you asking?"

"She's my sister." Her heart pounded. Hope soared he might have spotted Sadie.

The kid looked her up and down. "I ain't seen nobody."

Rhett took a step forward. "We're trying to find her. It's important. She's in danger."

Brice glanced around like searching for a way to bolt. Needle tracks dotted his arm. He jerked his sleeves down when he saw Brandi's gaze. "I didn't talk to her."

"But you saw her?" Brandi tried to keep her tone calm, afraid he'd stop talking.

The kid nodded. "There was a chick here."

"Come on, Brice. Spit out what you know." Rhett folded his arms. "I have nowhere else to go today." He glanced at Brandi with a cocked eyebrow.

She caught on. "Me, neither. I have all day."

Brice shuffled his feet. "I want to go home."

"Do your parents know you're shooting up?"

"They don't care what I do." He held his hands in the air. "Like I said. I didn't talk to her. But I saw a girl a couple of days ago with a kid. I hang out here sometimes when I want to be alone, and I saw a car parked behind the barracks."

"What kind of car?" Rhett asked.

Brandi found it difficult not to take over the conversation, but she had to admit Rhett was probably better at getting answers. If they knew what model of car Sadie was driving, that could be instrumental in locating her sister.

Brice shrugged. "I dunno. A small dark car with faded paint on the hood. Didn't have no hubcaps."

"Go on." Rhett nodded.

"I waited around until I saw who was in the bunk room. I heard that kid cry and then the lady walked by the window."

Brandi stepped forward. "How old was this kid? Was it a boy or girl?" As soon as the words were out, she wished she could take them back. The scowl on Brice's face warned her she was an unwanted intrusion.

Rhett must've sensed the teen's hostility and said, "Answer her."

"I dunno how old the boy was. Maybe one or two. I ain't good with kids."

"Did you talk to her?" Rhett continued. "Get her name?"

"Are you crazy? I already told you I didn't talk to her."

The guy obviously had stuff to hide and didn't want people to know he was here. Whether he'd run away from home, was dealing drugs or just using, he wanted to be invisible.

Brandi couldn't be quiet any longer. She said, "We have the little boy. We need to find his mama. She's in danger, and we want to help."

Brice stared at her. "You said she's your sister?"

"Yeah. I'm worried about her. Please help."

His defenses seemed to soften. "I don't know nothin' about her, but I watched to see what she was up to. That's when this big guy shows up. As soon as he walked into the barracks, she sprinted around the back of the building and ran to her car. She barely made it out of here."

Rhett asked, "What day was this?"

"The day before last in the middle of the night."

Rhett and Brandi exchanged glances. That was when Sadie called 911.

"What was the guy driving?"

Brice shrugged. "Some kind of large SUV. Older model and covered in mud. It was loud, like it didn't have a muffler." His head bobbed. "Kind of cool."

"Here's my number." Rhett handed him a business card. "Call me if you think of anything else."

"Okay." The kid glanced at Brandi one more time and then back to Rhett. "Am I free to go?"

"Yes," Rhett answered. "Can I give you a ride to your house?"

He chuckled. "Uh, no thanks. Wouldn't go too well if my dad seen me drive up with a Texas Ranger."

They waited for Brice to walk away, and then watched him turn south on the paved road.

Rhett said, "I'm willing to guess that's not the way to his house."

"I was thinking the same thing."

He started for the hangar when Brandi hollered over the wind, "Sadie was here, and I have proof."

"What's your proof?" He shook the chill off him. "Let's get out of the cold."

Brandi stayed by the door where the building blocked the wind. She knew Rhett didn't 100 percent buy that Levi's mom was Sadie, but she had to show him what she found. "Come with me."

Rhett looked back at her. "Where are you going?"

"I told you, I have proof. Sadie left me a message."

He strode her way and his eyebrows arched. "What message?"

She jerked her head toward the barracks. "I'd rather show you." After he stepped through the door, she continued, "I didn't see it at first, but one of the writings on the wall said, 'I love me, too.'" She went on to explain how she and Sadie used with the phrase to banter with each other.

He seemed to consider what she said. "Brandi, why do you believe Sadie doesn't call you? Where do you think she's been for the last two years?"

"I've asked myself those questions a thousand times. I honestly don't know."

"What does your instinct tell you?"

She sighed. *Wishful thinking.* That was what she feared. That her imagination was running amok with false hope. "I'm afraid she's dead, but in my gut, deep down, I think she's alive and in trouble. I don't know where's she been or why she hasn't called, but whatever the reason, she had no choice."

"Fair enough."

She was glad he hadn't argued. Quarreling with him would be too much with her emotions on a roller coaster. It was *almost* as if Rhett was on her side. But she couldn't even depend on family or the people she'd grown up with.

She shivered and hurried up to the second floor. Temperatures seemed to be dropping, and not wanting to waste time, Brandi pointed out the graffiti left by her sister. "Right there."

Rhett moved over to the wall and examined the floor. After a few moments, he snapped a few photos with his cell phone, and then took more pictures of the floor and other walls even though Brandi doubted the other graffiti was created by her sister.

He slipped his phone back into the belt holder. "Did you find anything else?"

"No. But I'm certain if we check the footprints, there's actually two different sets. One belonging to Brice and one to Sadie. I was on my way to check out this locker over here when Brice jumped out and scared me to death."

"I'll look." He stepped across the debris and pulled the door back. "It's empty. I don't think there's anything else."

"Good, let's go." She rubbed her hands up and down her biceps. "It's getting colder."

Brandi hurried down the stairs with Rhett behind her. She walked down the long hallway and was about to open the front door when feet on gravel made her freeze.

"In here." A man's voice sounded by the door.

She and Rhett looked at each other, their gazes locked for a split second. No time to run back upstairs.

"This way," Rhett whispered, tugging on her sleeve and dashed for the open doorway. They stepped onto the stairs leading down into the air raid shelter as the front door opened.

Brandi's whole body quivered. One step in this direction, and they'd be spotted.

Rhett put his finger to his lips, encouraging her to be quiet, and then pointed down.

Into the freezing water? No way!

Several footsteps clambered into the room.

How many men were there? Panic crawled up her throat.

"Where is she?" a man's scratchy voice echoed.

Brandi's foot searched for the next step, and her toe touched brick. Frigid water engulfed her.

"Up there."

"You go check it out. See if she left anything behind. Joe, check the hangar and check it good. I'll look around here."

Movement continued around the room.

Rhett slid into the water and took her arm, guiding her deeper into the bitter darkness. He withdrew his Glock from his holster.

Her whole body trembled as she fought to keep herself from panicking. Leaves and filth floated among the thin slivers of ice and brushed against her arm. The cold squeezed her chest, sucking the breath from her body.

Please, Lord, help me to remain calm. I can't go any deeper. I'll panic. Help me not to panic!

With her hand still in his, Rhett took another step down. "I've got you. Trust me."

She whispered, "Can't you shoot our way out?"

He shook his head and mouthed, "Too many."

Terror rose in her throat, but with Rhett's encouragement, her foot descended another step. The water came up to her neck. Cold stuck like tiny needles and her lungs tightened with each breath. Brandi's body instantly shook. She was barely aware of Rhett as he went even further down the pitch-black tunnel. What would these guys do if they found them? No doubt Rhett's pistol couldn't hold them all off.

Just as footsteps headed their way, Rhett pulled her under the surface. His arms went round her waist, tugging her close.

Mentally, she screamed. Her gaze searched the surface for light—anything to keep the terror at bay, but darkness swallowed them. The blind spot in her eye made it even more difficult to see clearly. Her world closed in. She jerked her arm, needing to be free from Rhett's restraining grasp.

His hold held firm. A hand rubbed her back, evidently trying to soothe her.

Please God, help me to calm down. I don't want to die.

She closed her eyes. *Relax. Relax.* Her brain repeated the word. She had begun to get control of her thoughts when Rhett pulled her even deeper and the brick pressed against her side. Her eyes flew open.

A bright light appeared beside her.

Rhett's gun pointed up from his side.

The guy had a flashlight, and the light illuminated the surface. Could he see them? Did the thin broken layer of ice give away their hiding place?

She tried not to fight Rhett's tug, but she couldn't hold out any longer. Her lungs burned. Fireflies danced before her eyes. She was going to pass out. Maybe it'd be better that way.

Suddenly, hands shoved her upward. She and Rhett crested the water at the same time. She fought with everything in her being not to cough. She drew deep, measured breaths.

Her toes and legs stung. She searched out Rhett in the murky water. He, too, sucked air, but didn't make a sound. Noise and movement scuffled in the big room. How long could they survive in this watery grave?

Rhett positioned himself in front of her—she supposed to protect her if shots were fired. He whispered in her ear, "Are you okay?"

"Freezing," she returned the whisper. "I can't stay in here any longer. Can you use your gun?"

"They have assault rifles. Stay close. We'll get out of here in a little bit."

She'd never been so cold in her life. Rhett slid his Glock into his holster and wrapped his arms around her. As much as she appreciated it, the gesture brought no relief. He was freezing, too.

Rhett dropped his chin to the top of her head. His

warm breath felt good on her cheek, and she sagged against him. If they ever got out of here alive, she intended to tell him how much he had meant to her.

Clang.

The sound echoed in the other room. Then a door opened and shut. At least one person had gone outside.

Please, let the rest of them leave.

Finally, fast walking boots moved across the floor.

Good. Maybe they were all going.

In a baritone voice, one of the men asked, "Did you find anyone?"

"Nope. Neither one of 'em."

Neither of them? Were they hoping to find her and Sadie? Her and Rhett? She didn't recognize either voice.

"They must've left already. I told you Joe was driving too slowly. Stupid old man."

"Shut up. He's not that old." The second guy had a high-pitched voice and talked fast like he was nervous. "You're the one that kept searching the house for your gun, and it was in the truck the whole time."

"Yeah, well, the boss ain't gonna be happy."

"Let's get back to the station," the nervous man said. "The sheriff can't know we're here."

The sheriff? Brandi glanced at Rhett and she could see the wheels turning in his head. His jaws were clenched. From the cold or anger, she did not know.

The two men went out the door.

"Follow me."

Brandi would like nothing better than to get out of this hole, but what if the guys came back in?

As if he read her thoughts, Rhett said, "Come on. You can wait on the steps while I make certain they are gone."

Her whole body was numb. When her foot stepped on

the next step, her shoe slipped and she slid back under, the water engulfing her. She gulped a mouthful.

An attempt to regain balance went nowhere. Her muscles refused to work.

Strong hands grabbed her by the arm and tugged her up. She gasped for air. The men would hear her if they returned, but she couldn't control the spasms.

"I've got you, Brandi. You're safe." He gave her a little shake. "Brandi. Can you hear me?"

She willed herself to concentrate on his words. The stinging needles didn't hurt as bad. Her legs were noodles. No matter how hard she tried, she couldn't maintain her balance.

Then she was falling.

"Brandi." His voice grew fainter.

Rhett's arms quivered with muscle fatigue as he hoisted Brandi out of the water and placed her on the floor next to the top step. Hypothermia would set in soon if it hadn't already.

He had to get Brandi warm, and quickly.

With his clothes plastered to him and dripping with water, he shook uncontrollably. Eliciting strength from pure desperation, he dragged her a couple of feet from the edge so she wouldn't fall back in.

A glance out the door showed a white Suburban pulling out of the drive with the brown-and-white Ford Bronco behind it. Rhett didn't wait to make certain they were gone before he moved back to Brandi.

She was curled into a fetal position and shaking viciously. Her lips had taken on a blue tint; her teeth chattered.

His heartbeat raced, nearly exploding, as he'd never seen Brandi this feeble.

They needed to get out of their wet clothes. Rhett ripped off his jacket and shirt but left on his white T-shirt. As dirty as the blanket was on the second floor, it would have to do. No time to worry about a little grime. He attempted to run, but his legs simply wouldn't comply. With extraordinary effort, he reached the top of the stairs, snatched the ragged blanket and returned to Brandi's side. "Let's get you out of your coat."

When he ripped away the coat, he noticed a small patch of black under her sweatshirt. Thankfully, she had dressed in layers and wore a black thermal top under her blouse.

He'd dealt with victims of hypothermia and knew it was important to get her out of the soggy clothes. Her hands were shaking so badly he had to help her get the sweatshirt over her head. He draped the blanket around her. "I'll be right back."

She nodded.

Rhett trudged across the lot and around the back of the hangar to his truck, numbness making his legs feel like bricks. A flick of his hand had the heat on high, and he drove the truck over to the barracks. Hurrying back inside, he scooped Brandi into his arms. Wooziness overtook him.

He fell against the wall. *Curse this weakness.*

Sucking in a breath, he carried her to the passenger side. Once she was settled, he laid the seat back and removed her shoes and thick socks.

She grimaced.

"Sorry." He tucked the blanket securely around her.

"I know it's cold, but we'll have you warm in a few minutes."

She didn't say a word but continued to shiver.

With two fingers, he checked her pulse. Weak and slow. It scared him half to death seeing her like this.

His toes were numb. He hated to take time to remove his boots and socks, but the chance of hypothermia was simply too great. As he slid off his boots, pain shot through his feet and legs. He placed his gun on the console to dry. The heater blew hot air through the cab and floor vents.

As the blood warmed in his veins, his toes burned like fire.

Brandi needed medical care. He'd never seen her so pale. But how safe would they be at the hospital? There'd be little protection, and they'd be vulnerable to attack.

"How are you doing?"

She kept her arms tight around herself. "Freezing."

His place was thirty minutes closer than Pam's or the hospital, so he turned left.

No, he'd have to take a chance and bring her to the hospital. The medical staff could administer warm saline through intravenous therapy or could rewarm her blood if needed.

The temptation to call his uncle or the local police kept flitting through his mind. He and Brandi needed help. But his stomach tightened into a ball at the thought. Could he trust them? Why had the gunman mentioned the sheriff?

Mulberry Gap PD had a good working relationship with Jarvis County Sheriff's Department and communicated often. Even if he called the police chief, the chance of Chief Tom Bradshaw notifying his uncle was great.

A white vehicle appeared in his rearview mirror a

half mile behind. From this distance, he couldn't tell if it was a truck or an SUV. Goose bumps covered his skin. His muscles cramped, and his fingers and toes had lost all feeling.

Being confronted now put them at a huge disadvantage.

Holes littered the paved road, preventing him from speeding, but he accelerated a little more. As the vehicle gained on them, he realized it was a Suburban.

Please, be a lady with a car full of kids returning home from seeing Santa Claus and not one of the men from the airfield.

He hit Luke's number on his Bluetooth. "I need backup. Can you come to Mulberry Gap?"

"I can be out the door in ten minutes, but it'll take me three or four hours to reach you."

The Suburban drew closer.

Luke asked, "What's the rundown?"

Rhett gave Luke the abbreviated version and then clicked off. The SUV was right on them. A sharp turn showed to the right. He kept his speed until the junction appeared in front of him. His barefoot slammed on the brakes and the truck skid through the turn.

The SUV flew past.

Using his advantage, he gassed it and increased the distance. A rock road appeared to his right, and he took it. The freezing weather kept the dust down, hopefully hiding his route. Chug holes filled the way, and he jerked the wheel back and forth to dodge them.

Brandi sat up. "Wha...what's going on?" Her words slurred.

"Hang on." He didn't want to scare her, but more important, he didn't want to get caught in the open in their condition. "The SUV from the airfield is following us."

She blinked like she was trying to clear her mind. After a few seconds, she laid her head back and closed her eyes. Confusion was a symptom of hypothermia.

In the distance, the SUV appeared again in his mirror. A decrepit house surrounded by cedar trees emerged at the bottom of the hill. He increased his speed. When he was almost there, he hit his brakes and jerked the wheel. The truck jolted over the rough terrain and tore down the overgrown drive.

Hopefully, they were too far away for the driver to see him turn.

Rhett drove behind the house and under the branches of an enormous cedar tree. Several limbs broke as the vehicle brushed against the trunk. He killed the engine. They were well hidden.

Brandi mumbled, "Where are we?"

"Hiding from the guys from the airfield." Rhett continued to watch for the SUV.

She frowned. "That's not good."

"No, it's not." He found a couple of napkins in the console and rubbed down his gun until it was good and dry. He fumbled to put in new bullets.

Suddenly, splashes of white shone between the branches as the SUV drove by the house. Brake lights came on, followed by backup lights.

Oh no.

"Brace yourself. The guy is coming our way."

She nodded and grabbed the handle above the door.

A few seconds later, the vehicle whipped down the drive and around the house. The roar of the engine amplified in the silence.

Rhett held his breath. The cedar trees mostly concealed them, but if the man saw the truck, an escape would be impossible without gunfire.

A shed sat twenty yards in front of their position. The Suburban belted for the crumbling outbuilding. Brake lights flashed as it came to a stop.

He squeezed Brandi's hand. "Don't move."

"Is he coming?" Her voice broke and came out too loud.

"No, not yet," he whispered.

The SUV continued to sit there. Rhett could imagine the man was taking a good look.

Did his truck reflect through the trees?

The man backed up the vehicle before tearing out of the property.

As soon as he was gone, Rhett started the truck. For a couple of minutes, they sat there quietly with the heat running, waiting to make sure the guy didn't return. Finally, when Rhett knew the coast was clear, he pulled out on the road. The man had continued north on the rock road, so Rhett turned south.

Brandi's eyes were closed again, her face still extremely pale.

Plans had changed. Going to the hospital would increase the chance of being pursued again. Brandi needed to get warm. And there was only one place close by that he could take her. He took the next dirt road on his left and after a few miles, turned right.

He followed the winding, rough road for twelve minutes before turning into the drive of a large pasture. He opened the barbwire gate, drove through and closed it again. Heads of the white Brahman cattle came up as the animals watched them cross the open field to the back of the property. The cabin could barely be seen in the thick foliage, and small seedlings littered the unused path. His truck bounced across a couple of washouts before coming to a stop by the building.

There was no garage or carport. No electric poles but power came from a generator.

Brandi looked up. "Where are we? I thought we were going to your house." Her words were sluggish.

"To the cabin."

"What cabin? I don't understand."

"Don't worry about it right now. We just needed somewhere safe to stay." *The cabin where I proposed to you.*

It was painful, but he slid on his boots and then stepped around the truck to help her inside.

"Oh. Oh. My feet are stinging." She cringed as she attempted to walk across the stepping-stones like it was a sticker patch.

"Hold on." After securing the key from under the river rock by the back door, he unlocked the back door, leaving it ajar.

"Here, I've got you." His feet tingled, too, but not as badly as when they first came out of the freezing water. He scooped up Brandi, carried her inside and placed her on the couch. Dust covered everything, and the temperatures were the same as outside.

"I'll be right back." He hurried out the door and started the generator. An extra container full of gasoline sat beside the house, ensuring several days' worth of power. When he returned inside, he climbed up the steep stairs to the loft. He grabbed two pairs of thick pants, men's fleece sweatshirts, socks and a couple of more blankets from a trunk.

He brought a set of clothes to her. "Can you put these on?"

With her eyes closed, she nodded. "Get out."

"Um. The bathroom's that way."

"What?" She glanced around. Her eyes squinted at her surroundings. "Where are we? This place looks…"

He didn't want her worrying about where they were and gave her a nudge. "Go change out of your wet clothes while I get a fire going."

Uncertainty crossed her face. "Okay."

Swiftly, he peeled out of his clothes to make certain he beat her getting dressed. He shivered from the chill and dabbed himself dry with a towel before shrugging into dry clothes.

A thud came from the bathroom.

"Are you all right?" He moved to the door, ready to open it in case she'd fallen.

"I'm fine." Her voice held a twinge of annoyance. "I was shaking so bad I lost my balance when I tried to get these stupid jeans off."

He couldn't hold back a smile. Brandi sounded like her normal self, which gave him hope she'd be okay once the cabin was warm. A box of starter logs lay on top of the pile of wood beside the woodburning stove. By the time she came out of the bathroom, he had the fire going.

"These clothes are too big." She held out the side of the pants leg. "Who do they belong to?"

"No one in particular. There were extra clothes in a trunk in the loft." The rancher who owned the place had built the cabin for his wife. The retired couple had lived in Dallas and enjoyed staying in the cabin, coming in to check on the cattle on weekends. His wife had kept the place well stocked with extra clothes and food in case somebody dropped by. While in training at the academy, Rhett had worked on the ranch part-time and could use the cabin anytime he wanted. After the man's wife died, the rancher never used it again, but had left a standing offer to Rhett.

Exhaustion consumed Rhett, but he needed to take care of Brandi first. He was glad she hadn't recognized the place.

Her face wrinkled up as she stared out one of the tall glass walls. "Are we at the cabin?"

So much for that thought. He didn't want to deal with this conversation right now. The structure had two glass walls that gave an awesome view of the trees and the creek, but also made the place easy to distinguish.

"Yes, we are. It was the closet safe place." He walked over with a dry quilt. "Lie down on the couch."

She did as he asked and pulled the quilt to her chin. "I'm freezing."

"The room will be warm in a bit." He turned on the heat and padded into the tiny kitchen. He rinsed out the coffee pot before putting on a pot, and then opened a can of chicken broth and divided it between two cups. After two minutes in the microwave, he brought her a cup. "Drink this."

"Don't want it." She held up her hand and turned her face away.

"Brandi, it's important you get some warm liquids in you." When she didn't respond, he retrieved a thermometer from the first aid box and scanned her forehead. Ninety-four. "Wake up. Your temperature is too low. I need you to sit up and drink this."

"I just want to sleep."

"You can in a bit, but let's get you warmed up first."

She struggled to a sitting position.

"Here." He held the mug to her lips.

She took a big swig and spilled it on her chin.

"Easy. Just sip it." With his help, she finally drank half of a cup.

She swiped her mouth with the back of her hand. "That tastes good."

"Excellent." When she had finished drinking, he leaned back on the couch and consumed his broth, savoring the warmth.

He grabbed one of the fleece blankets from the closet and tossed it into the stackable dryer. With a stab from the poker, flames kicked up higher in the stove, making it feel warmer. He retrieved the hot blanket a few minutes later and exchanged it for Brandi's.

Her breathing had leveled out. He checked her pulse again, and found it was stronger and not as slow. Some color had returned to her skin, as well.

He tossed their wet clothes in the dryer. Feeling drained, he sat in the chair and covered up with another throw. Because of his larger size, the cold should affect him less compared to someone Brandi's size. He leaned back, intending to rest but for a minute.

The trees blew and leaves kicked up in the breeze outside of the cabin. This place was well hidden, and the glass walls offered an awesome view of the goings-on outside.

But that also meant anyone could see in, making it impossible for them to completely hide.

ELEVEN

Brandi awoke. She glanced around, trying to get her bearings. The room was dark, and the sound of wood popping in the stove caught her attention.

Levi. Where was Levi?

The woodstove wasn't familiar, nor the decorations that glowed on the mantel. Her gaze landed on the shadowy figure in the recliner. Rhett.

Memories came flooding back. Parker Airfield. The black tunnel. Frigid water. Not being able to breathe. And the man gazing into the water.

Where was Levi? She let out a breath of relief as she remembered her nephew was safely being watched by Pam.

Sadie had left the message in the barracks.

Brandi sat up. "Rhett. We have to find Sadie."

The Ranger jumped, his arms going in the air. "Huh?"

"It's me. Brandi." She'd been so out of it she couldn't remember what all happened after she got out of the water. Rhett had helped her. He'd been in the same freezing temperatures as she. "Are you okay?"

He glanced around, still looking dazed. "What's wrong?" He stood, the blanket falling to the ground, and he grabbed his gun from the end table. "Is someone here?"

"No. No. No. I don't think so." She hadn't meant to startle him, but evidently, he'd been sound asleep. "I just woke. What time is it?"

"Seven thirty." Alarm registered on his face, and he kicked the blanket out of his way. "I can't believe I dozed off."

He grabbed his gun and glanced out the glass walls. "It's dark outside. I'll be right back." He stared at his bare feet and then strode behind the recliner. "I need my boots."

"Let me turn on a light so you can see better."

"No. Don't touch the switch."

"Why not?" His loud voice startled her, making her flinch.

"Let me check things out first."

"Okay." Her hand went to her throat as she tried to clear the cobwebs. There was clomping as he put on his shoes and then the door opened and shut.

These clothes weren't hers. Why was she wearing men's clothing? Where had Rhett put her clothes? A check in the tiny bathroom where she'd changed showed nothing. Of course, it was even darker in there.

"Everything's clear," he called out. He came into the room, turned on the light, and took one glance at her. "Would you like your clothes? I threw them in the dryer."

"Thanks. I would." Now that he was awake, he moved quickly. Brandi knew he didn't like falling asleep while she needed protecting. The stackable washer and dryer were positioned under the stairs to the loft.

When he returned with her clothes, she attempted to appease him. "Everything is all right."

He didn't pretend not to understand what she meant. "I know. But I shouldn't have fallen asleep. If those men had found us…"

"But they didn't. The cold water zapped your energy, too. I may not be in law enforcement, Rhett, but I know one of the symptoms of hypothermia is extreme fatigue."

He swiped the thermometer from the counter and took her temperature. "It's 97.2. How are you feeling?"

"Weak."

"From what you've been through, I'd say that is expected. Let me see your arm."

She held it out and he placed his fingers on her wrist.

He listened and then said, "Your pulse is strong. Let me know if you begin to feel worse."

Another look around and she realized this one-room house looked familiar. But that was impossible. Except— she glanced around one more time and gasped. "You brought me to the cabin?"

His head dropped to the side. "Yes. I had no other option. I told you this earlier."

"There's always an option." Hurt and betrayal descended on her. Why would he take her to the place that had been such a part of their past? "I don't want to be here."

"Brandi, I didn't have an option. I would've preferred to have taken you to the hospital." His gaze was stoic and stern.

The hospital. Yes, she was in bad shape. She swallowed back the turmoil rumbling through her stomach. But the cabin?

If she never saw the place again, it would please her fine. There were too many memories. Good memories. The running creek contained catfish and had once been a staple fishing hole for her and Rhett. When he worked on the ranch while they were dating, she would pick up fast food on Friday nights, and they'd enjoy eating and fishing under the stars. The cabin was the perfect spot because there were restrooms and it had heating and air-conditioning. Not exactly roughing it. When Rhett worked later than planned, she had a comfy place to wait—if she didn't wind up helping him work cattle.

A smile crossed her lips. She supposed since her grandparents lived on a farm, she had learned to appreciate the animals.

Then, on a spring Sunday afternoon after worship services, he'd taken her to this ranch with a metal detector under the pretext of looking for antique junk by a nearby old homeplace site. Brandi loved searching for treasures, and had dressed in her ratty denim shorts, an old T-shirt and running shoes. A storm blew in, and they'd run for the cover of the cabin. The lightning show was spectacular through the glass walls and the pounding rain had made her feel miles away from any other human.

And then Rhett had dropped to his knee and produced a ring.

Moisture filled her eyes. She didn't want to remember those times—pleasant, carefree times. It wasn't real. Love wasn't real. Aside from God, she was alone.

Stop it, Brandi. The cabin *was* on the northwestern side of the county, close to Parker Airfield. Her heart raced, and she tried to slow the rapid pace.

"Are you okay?" Rhett stepped forward and placed his hands on her shoulders. He wiped a tear from her eye. "Hey…"

His touch sent electricity through her, and she shrugged away, breaking contact.

"I'm sorry." His gaze locked onto hers, but she turned her eyes to the floor. "Please don't cry. I never intended to hurt you."

"You didn't hurt me!" No one could hurt her. She spun back to him and wanted to lash out. Nothing made her want to cry more than someone telling her not to. *Rein in the weakness. Don't let him see you vulnerable.* It must be the near-death experience causing her to react foolishly.

"Brandi." He again stepped close, and his head dipped as he maneuvered so he could see her face. "I shouldn't have brought you here. I couldn't think of a safer place."

This time she couldn't look away from the intensity of his dark eyes. Several silent seconds ticked by with neither saying a word.

Their gazes remained locked as he moved in, his lips softly pressing against her forehead. She wanted nothing more than to melt into his embrace, to feel his strong, secure arms around her. But she couldn't—wouldn't. She took a step back, knocking a book off the coffee table in the process. "Don't. I can't…"

"Sorry." He ran his fingers through his hair. "I hate seeing you this way."

"Don't worry about me." The conversation needed to be changed. "I'm more concerned about finding Sadie. If those men find her, she won't have a chance."

The stern set of his chin said his concern was for her. "You still look weak."

"I'm fine and am ready to go."

"We're staying here until morning." He said it like there was no debate.

"Don't start telling me what I'm allowed to do."

He sighed, and his shoulders slumped. "I'd never tell

you what to do unless it was necessary. You know me better than that, Callahan. Trust me."

Rhett worried about her because he cared. That much she knew was true, even if it put undue pressure on her. Why did she feel guilty for ending their relationship when it was he who had caused her to lose faith in people?

Suddenly the vehicle chasing them came to her mind. She'd been so out of it that the memories were slow to return. "What happened when we left the airfield? Did someone chase us?"

"One of the gunmen followed us in a white Suburban. Do you know anyone who drives one?"

"Mrs. Watkins, and, uh, Mrs. Choate. Both have several kids and are married to nice guys."

"So neither family seems like the murdering kind?"

She laughed. "Not likely." She sobered as more recollections came to her. "Did you hide your truck in a tree?"

"Not in." He smiled. "*Under* a cedar tree."

She remembered now. The SUV had chased them down a back road and then driven up to their hiding place. "If that guy had seen us, we would've been sitting ducks."

"I'd say so."

Brandi had refused to lean on anyone over the past couple of years. She'd been stubborn, if only for her own good. The fear of being betrayed ruled her actions and kept her from believing in anyone.

Trust me. Rhett's words replayed through her mind. If only he knew what it took from her to agree to the simple request.

Difficult to admit, but she never would've survived the last couple of days without help. Even if she'd escaped injury when her car dangled over the ravine, she never could've fought off the men at the airfield.

To her very core, it petrified her to rely on others. But if she were going to find Sadie and restore her family's reputation, she couldn't do it without the man standing in front of her.

"I'll trust you. Don't let me down."

Rhett still couldn't believe Brandi had said she'd trust him. What an enormous step that was for her.

God, please help me to not let her down.

After she said the words, she'd changed back into her own clothes, grabbed a snack and remained quiet, appearing deep in thought. Brandi wouldn't regret believing in him. If it was the last thing he did, he intended to keep her safe.

He, too, changed back into jeans and his own clothes. Securing his gun and phone, he was about to yell out he was going outside to perform a walk around but saw that she had settled back on the couch.

He stepped onto the front deck that overhung the creek. The cedar trees were mature and tall, heavy with limbs, providing excellent cover for them.

And a secure hiding place for anyone who might be out there.

A slow walk around the structure didn't show any signs of human prints. Only occasional markings of birds or those of a rabbit. Sleet was firm, hiding movement better than snow. But there were still places soft enough to show a man's passage. No such spot could he find on the ground tonight. Maybe they had lost the man earlier today. Few knew of this cabin.

Rhett's cell rang, and he answered on the first ring. "Hey, Luke. Where are you?"

"At the Mulberry Gap Bed and Breakfast's parking lot. Do I need to check in or meet you somewhere?"

"Brandi and I are safe at a cabin for the moment, on the northwest side of town. So yeah, I need you to stay there and keep an eye out for a white Suburban and an older-model brown-and-white Ford Bronco."

"License plate numbers?"

"Didn't get those." Rhett had already given him the lowdown on what happened at the airfield. "Oh, I almost forgot. Also let me know if you spot a dark, small car with a faded hood and no hub caps. The kid at the airfield described the car he thought Sadie was driving."

"That's a good tip."

"Yeah. I hope that one pans out." Rhett wasn't certain he should mention the sheriff's department. He knew better than to accuse another law agency, but then Luke knew how to handle things delicately. "Let me know if you notice any suspicious activity from the sheriff's department."

Silence radiated through the call.

"It's a hunch, but someone from the department may be involved. Before the gunmen left the airfield, one mentioned going back to the station. So far, there's three men who've participated in the attacks on Brandi. I don't believe any of them is calling the shots."

"That's easy to buy, considering over a million dollars is missing."

Rhett knew Luke would understand. "Stay low and out of sight. I'll call you tomorrow."

"Any word on the deputy that was shot?"

Rhett said, "No change since my last update."

"Okay. I'll take that as a good thing." A pause. "Be careful, Kincaid. And I don't mean from the gunmen."

Rhett quirked his lips and shook his head. "Tomorrow."

After he hung up, he walked the perimeter once more before stepping back into the house. Brandi had fallen asleep on the couch. Rhett had worked on a couple of cases with Luke Dryden, one right after Brandi had broken their engagement. Luke had seen how hurt he'd been. But things were different now. No one needed to worry that he'd jump back into a relationship with Brandi, even though he still cared for her. A lot.

The pain had shocked him when she'd left. But the knife to the heart was the fact that she didn't even attempt to work things out. How could she promise forever one minute and then drop him like a hot potato the next?

His dad had been fickle to leave their family that way. He had no compassion for anyone but himself. Rhett and Pam had been so young. Even if his parents' marriage hadn't worked out, it didn't mean his father couldn't spend time with his own children. But David Kincaid had given them nothing. No child support. No visits. Nada. Zilch.

Later, Rhett had heard his dad was in Kansas, working a factory job and moved in with a woman who had three small children. Supposedly, after four years, he'd left her along with his gambling debts and a pile of bills. Rhett hadn't received word from his dad since.

Didn't people realize the damage broken commitments caused?

Brandi's blond hair cascaded across her forehead, a stray strand blowing slightly with each breath. Rhett's chest rose with an intake of air. Yeah, he missed Brandi

Callahan being a part of life. The fun they used to have. Even though he'd gone on a couple of dates with other women, they couldn't compare to how she made him feel.

"Why are you frowning?" Brandi sat up and stretched.

"You're awake." Caught with his hand in the cookie jar. He was glad she couldn't read his thoughts. "Just mulling over everything."

She yawned and then looked at him again. "Couldn't have been good thoughts, with that look on your face."

"No, they weren't." Time to change the subject. "How are you feeling?"

"Better."

Color had returned to her face, and she appeared to be her normal self. "What about your hands and feet?"

She held up her hands, looked them over and shrugged. "Fine."

He walked over to the couch and motioned. "Let me see your feet."

"Yes, sir." She laughed and stuck them in the air and rolled her feet back and forth at the ankles.

Inwardly, he rolled his eyes, but didn't give her the satisfaction of openly responding. He inspected her feet, paying special attention to the toes. With a pinch of his fingers on her big toe, he asked, "Can you feel that?"

She flinched. "Yes, thank you."

He barely squeezed the baby toe. "What about here?"

"Mostly. Barely tingles and is a little uncomfortable."

That was what he thought. It wasn't uncommon for the hands and feet to suffer the most damage after being in freezing temperatures for a prolonged time. The color was white, with no bruises or black color—evidence of frostbite. That was good.

"I'm exhausted, like I could sleep all night. I know I shouldn't."

"Sleep is a good idea. Your body needs the rest." He didn't want to take chances with her health. The cabin was nearer the hospital in Blue Springs than the one in Mulberry Gap. And if anyone were looking for them, Mulberry Gap would be the first place they'd check.

"Sadie was at Parker Airfield. We have to find her."

"We will."

"When? 'We will' is not good enough."

He could tell by the stubborn set of her chin that he would not be able to put her off without a good reason. "I called Pam. She's good to keep Levi with her."

"Good." Brandi nodded. "I figured she would. Your sister has always been a caring person."

"Thanks. And I think we should go see your grandma tomorrow."

She blinked. "Grandma?" Her face fell. "Wait. You don't think she has anything to do with the stolen money?"

He took a seat in the recliner and cocked his head at her.

"Grandma?" She shouted the word in disbelief and tossed her hands in the air. "Seriously?"

He held his hand up. "I'm not saying your grandma— or anyone else in your family—had anything to do with stealing the money, but the farm would be the perfect hiding place. More important, Sadie may've been in touch with her."

Brandi clasped her chest and shook her head. "Might want to lay the groundwork next time before you spit out an accusation like that. I see what you're saying."

He glanced at the clock. "It's after nine. Too late to

see her tonight. Get a good night's rest, make sure you're recuperated for tomorrow and we'll go in the morning."

She nodded. "Do you really think Sadie may've contacted my grandma at the assisted-living place?"

"Your sister called you and left Levi in your care."

Brandi seemed to consider this. Rhett understood the constant battle of trying to figure out why Sadie hadn't called again or returned for her son. His greatest fear was that someone had killed Brandi's sister after she made the 911 call. He prayed that not be the case, for Brandi's sake.

One down and one to go.

The words kept running through his mind. But if so, the man's intent was to exterminate Brandi.

A game of cat and mouse.

The next move belonged to Rhett. He prayed he wasn't reading the game wrong.

TWELVE

Brandi wondered if it had been a mistake not to call to let her grandma know she and Rhett were coming for a visit.

What if Grandma was having a bad day or was asleep? The older woman wasn't suffering from dementia, but it had been a couple of months since Brandi had seen her. After falling and breaking her hip last year while getting ready for their Christmas family get-together, Grandma had gone straight from the hospital to rehab, and then to the nursing home where she lived now. The few times Grandma had called, Brandi had been busy and cut the conversation short.

Guilt tugged at Brandi's conscience as Rhett pulled down the street to the facility. She stared out the window, not wanting him to read the shame on her face. She should've been more diligent in checking on her dad's mom—the woman who had always supported and listened to her while she was growing up. Brandi's rough and tough personality aligned more with her grandmother's than her own mother's soft and gentle ways.

Brandi's relationship with her mom had never been all that great and had suffered even more when her mom started dating Phil Sandford. Now, with Dad and Sadie gone, Brandi was left with just her grandma.

"We're here."

"We made good time." She glanced around at the parking lot. "No one followed us?"

He shook his head. "I kept an eye out."

She had figured that much.

Rhett shoved his Stetson on his head. She liked the way he looked in his hat and had always appreciated rugged men. Though she stole another glance, she had to admit that no matter how tempting the scenery, she didn't have time to dwell on the Ranger's appealing qualities when someone wanted her dead.

They headed through the glass door into the lobby. Flowery sofas and outdated blue carpeting greeted them at the door. Even though the entrance appeared clean and well maintained, it didn't compare to the warmth and comfort of Grandma's home. Brandi tried to shove away the melancholy. Too much had changed in so little time.

Rhett followed behind her as she headed down the hall.

A lady seated behind a huge circular counter glanced up and smiled. Her name tag read Tasha. "May I help you?"

"We're here to see my grandma. Estelle Callahan."

"Oh, more visitors," Tasha beamed. "Mrs. Estelle will love that. She's been in the recreation hall for the last forty minutes. I'll need to see your picture identifications and you both need to sign in."

Brandi and Rhett exchanged glances as they pulled out their driver's licenses and filled out the form. When they were finished and had walked out of hearing distance, Brandi said, "I tried to get a look on the sign-in sheet to see who had visited, but it was a clean paper."

"I noticed that, too." He put his hand on the small of her back as they moved into the recreation room.

Her grandmother sat at a table with three other people, dominoes stacked in front of each of them.

"Grandma." Brandi shot her a smile.

"Oh, my." Her grandmother beamed. "Come over here." She stood and pulled her into a hug. After they released each other, she took Brandi's hand and faced the table. "This is my granddaughter Brandi."

Inwardly, Brandi grimaced. Talk about a guilt trip. She must force her conscience to the back of her mind until Sadie was found. Then she would make plans to spend more time with her grandmother.

"Hello," the two women replied in unison. Brandi recognized them from her previous visit.

The only man at the table looked up through thick, black-rimmed glasses. "She's even more beautiful than you described, Estelle."

"Smart, too, Henry." Grandma glanced over Brandi's shoulder. "Is that Rhett Kincaid hiding behind you? Haven't seen him in a long time."

"Yes, ma'am." When she threw her arms around his neck, Rhett hugged her back, lifting her off the ground a bit. "It's good to see you again. I haven't played forty-two since the last time at your house."

"You play?" Henry went to stand. "You can have my seat, young man."

Brandi held up her hand. "That's okay. Maybe next time. We need to talk with you, Grandma."

"Of course." Her grandmother glanced across the

room to a white-haired woman knitting in the corner. "Dorothy. Come take my place."

The older woman clapped her hands. "About time. We're going to put Henry and Fannie away."

The others at the table playfully challenged each other.

As they walked to her grandma's room, a strange feeling came over her. Brandi remembered Rhett coming over to her grandma's house and playing forty-two with the family. He had fit in so well. They'd begun dating not long after Grandpa died, and Grandma had liked Rhett immediately. He fell in with the family like he'd always belonged.

It didn't escape Brandi's attention that his hand went to the small of her back as he opened the door for her like it did while they were dating.

"Sorry, I have little room." Grandma picked up a newspaper from the couch and moved it to her nightstand. "We could sit on the patio if it weren't so nippy. I don't think this cold spell will ever end."

Nippy was putting it lightly. More like a blizzard in Texas terms. "It's okay, Grandma. The couch is fine. We can't stay long anyhow."

The sweet woman sat in the vinyl recliner beside the bed. Family photos dotted the walls. The double-wedding-ring quilt that had always been on her grandparents' bed covered the bed here. Sentimental knickknacks took up every available shelf.

"What brings you two by? By the looks on your faces, it's not just a friendly visit."

She smiled. "No, Grandma, I wished it were."

"Are you in some kind of trouble, honey?"

"Maybe." Brandi drew a deep breath. Grandma looked so gentle and concerned. So good. Brandi should've been visiting her more often than once a month. Rhett reached across the couch and gave Brandi's hand a little squeeze of encouragement. It helped to have him nearby. "I needed to ask you some questions about the farm. About Daddy and the family."

Her grandmother's smile faded. "All right, dear."

"I'm sure the authorities asked these questions many times, but do you remember anyone coming by the house the day he…well, you know." Her voice was suddenly dry. Even after two years, she still couldn't stand to say the words out loud.

"I'm afraid not. But like I told your mama, I was busy upstairs that day, finishing the quilt for Aubrey's baby before I left for the baby shower. I had been running myself ragged trying to get it done. I saw his car by the barn, but never saw him."

Aubrey was Brandi's cousin, and Brandi barely remembered her baby had been due at that time. With her father's death, nothing else in the world seemed to matter. Until Sadie went missing… She cleared her throat. "He never mentioned money?"

"Of course not. Your dad wasn't the kind to talk about personal things like that. He had been working with the chain saw earlier in the week, cutting up that large pecan tree that had split after a big storm. The tree was partially blocking my drive. I assumed he came to finish that day. It was funny because he'd called to say he wasn't coming by to work, but he came anyway."

The message he'd left on the machine had said as much.

"Your father was busy, but—" Grandma looked thoughtful "—he did seem…preoccupied. He was a quiet man, but I could still tell something was on his mind. Jordan was the best son a woman could ask for. After Richard passed, your father tried to keep up the farm while working at the bank."

Rhett sat silently and let her do all the talking. Having him there made the conversation easier.

Her grandmother took the questions well and seemed sharp as ever. But Brandi didn't want to upset her. "This might sound like a strange question, but have you heard from Sadie?"

Strangely, Grandma didn't seem surprised at all. "No, I haven't, but I've been thinking a lot about your sister lately. Do all these questions have to do with the man who visited me on Wednesday?"

Rhett and Brandi exchanged glances.

Her throat went dry. A man came by? "What man?"

Rhett leaned forward on the edge of the couch, placing his elbows on his knees. "Estelle, who came by to see you?"

"I don't remember his name, but it was the second time he stopped by." She held up her finger. "Wait. I have his name written down somewhere." She scrambled to her feet and opened the nightstand drawer.

"Grandma, what did he want?" Was it the bearded man who'd attacked Brandi at the barn? Or the guy who'd hit her with a board at the tin shed? Or maybe one of the men from the airfield? She got to her feet and went to stand beside her. "What did the man look like? Can you describe him?"

"Now, where did I put that slip of paper? I wrote his information on the back of an envelope." She slammed the top drawer of the nightstand shut and opened the bottom one.

Brandi couldn't fathom why someone would question

her grandmother. Unless they believed Grandma knew where the money was buried. *Buried?* Now, Brandi's thoughts had betrayed her. *There was no buried money!*

Her grandma planted her hands on her hips. "I made certain I put his information in a safe place because he asked me to call if I remembered anything else."

"Grandma." Brandi stood in front of her. "What did the man look like? Was he a big guy with a beard? In his fifties?"

"What? No. No. No. Average height. Probably in his forties, with a touch of gray around his temples. Sort of nice-looking and clean-cut, with a hint of a belly. If I had to guess, I'd say the man worked out but had a wife who was an excellent cook."

Grandma had always appreciated men with a healthy appetite and often complained about how scrawny the actors were on television. She claimed they'd never be able to complete a full day's work with so little meat on their bones.

Rhett moved beside Brandi. "Let me help you find the paper."

"Never mind. I found it." Grandma pulled out an envelope with writing scrawled across it from a bookshelf. "It was right there on top of my mail. John Graves is his name."

Brandi looked over Grandma's shoulder. Only a phone number besides the name. No title or business listed.

"Did he mention where he worked?" Rhett asked.

"I wouldn't give just anyone information." She planted her hands on her hips. "Let me think. He said something about an investigation. I think he was from the life insurance company."

"That makes no sense, Grandma." Brandi made certain to keep her voice calm even though panic swirled through her. "Daddy had insurance through his work, but they had refused to pay. Remember?"

"Oh, that's right." Grandma frowned and wrung her hands.

"Estelle, can you remember what he asked you?"

"Sure, young man. My memory hasn't failed me yet."

Even though Brandi feared her grandma might be flustered, she didn't appear so. Grandma looked Rhett directly in the eyes with her head held high. "He had questions about Jordan, the events surrounding his death, and then wanted to know about the rest of the family."

"What did you tell him?" Rhett's calm manner and smooth voice worked well to get people to open up. A trait Brandi appreciated unless it worked on her. She had always been free with her emotions around the man. Too much at times.

"Sure, but let's sit back down." After they returned to the couch and Grandma to the chair, she gave a brief narrative of the day Brandi's father had died, and the following weeks after the funeral. Then she picked back up with the conversation she had with her visitor.

Brandi listened intently, hoping her grandmother had shared nothing too personal with whoever this man was. His description didn't sound like the guy in the Bronco, but he could've been one of the others from the airfield. Brandi hadn't got a good look at any of them. "What did he want to know about us?"

"He asked if you or your mother had been spending a lot of money. Of course, I told him no. Except…"

"Except what?" Brandi leaned forward.

"Well, I explained how your mother is driving a new luxury SUV."

"But Phil bought her that vehicle."

"I told him that. Then John asked questions about your friends, Brandi. About your boyfriends. I told him about your breakup with Rhett. Of course, I didn't realize you two were back together."

Brandi went still and continued to stare straight ahead, forbidding her gaze to wander to Rhett. She had no desire to see him deny the relationship.

Rhett remained quiet, and Grandma continued. "He asked about the investigation into both Jordan's death and your sister's disappearance."

Rhett asked, "Can you remember specifically what he inquired about the investigation?"

"Just asked what the officers looked into. How long they investigated. Did they seem thorough? Don't worry, Rhett. I told them you had looked into Sadie's disappearance and I believed you did your best."

Did his best. *That made one of them.* The thought came instantly, and it surprised Brandi how easily she blamed Rhett for the unsuccessful probe into Sadie's disappearance and the failure to clear their family name.

What Grandma had to say about the man's visit was not what Brandi had expected. Why would someone ask about the investigation? What were they really after? Again, she and Rhett glanced briefly at each other. She couldn't read his mind but was eager to get his take.

She had intended to tell her grandmother about the emergency call from Sadie but reconsidered. Until Brandi knew the actual identity of Grandma's visitor and what he was after, information about Sadie's contacting her didn't need to be repeated.

Grandma frowned. "I suppose you heard about Deputy Norris getting shot."

If this John man had visited on Wednesday, he couldn't have known about the deputy yet. "Where did you hear that?"

"It's been on all the local news. A deputy gets shot at abandoned farm. What's this world coming to?"

"So no one asked you about the shooting?" Brandi didn't look at Rhett, but she could feel his eyes on her. The news must not have mentioned the location of the farm.

Her grandmother's face wrinkled up in concern. "Of course not. Why would they? My small group of friends have discussed it. Most people at this facility are from the area."

Brandi smiled. That made sense. *Please, Lord, help me not become paranoid.*

After another ten minutes, Brandi had learned nothing more, and Rhett spent his time on his phone. Brandi stood. "We need to be going."

"I enjoyed seeing you. Come back and bring that handsome man with you again." Grandma smiled. "I'm sure Sadie will come home soon."

An embarrassed smile crept across Brandi's face. What could she say that wouldn't make it sound like she thought Grandma had lost her faculties? And then there were the calls on the answering machine. "Oh, I know Sadie's missing. What about before you moved here, while you were still in your home? Did my sister call you after she'd left Mulberry Gap?"

Her grandmother clasped her hand and squeezed. "Oh no, Brandi. I would've told you if Sadie had called. Are you all right?"

"I'm fine." Brandi forced a smile. Either her elderly relative had never listened to Sadie's messages or had forgotten them. "Thanks again, Grandma." She gave her a hug and savored the scent of lavender. Tears prickled her eyes. A longing for the closeness they used to enjoy overwhelmed her.

With a quick swipe of hre eyes, Brandi murmured one last goodbye. She had to get out of here before she broke down.

A few minutes later, she and Rhett were pulling out of the parking lot.

He glanced are her. "Are you okay?"

"I'm fine." Now she felt silly for getting emotional. Recent events had taken their toll, causing her to be more sensitive—something she didn't particularly like. She looked at Rhett, who had concern written over his face. "What did you make of that? You think a man from the airfield paid Grandma a visit?"

"Nope." He shook his head. "Your grandma was paid a visit by the FBI."

Her mouth fell open. "They're looking into the case again?"

Maybe they would help find Sadie.

The man asked if you or your mother had been spending a lot of money. Her stomach tightened into a ball.

Could the FBI be looking into Phil's bank accounts?

Or maybe Brandi would be framed for stealing a million dollars.

Rhett noticed the stunned and worried expression on Brandi as soon as he mentioned the FBI. Not that he blamed her. When Luke had told him about John Graves's identity, he'd been surprised, too. Why was the FBI investigating now? Had something recently come up on their radar? Or had they been silently working the case the whole time?

A million dollars was a large sum of money and would keep the case active.

He turned left at the red light and checked his mirror. No one was tailing them that he could tell. Things were starting to come together. They didn't have the answers, but it felt like the case was about to blow wide open. Another Texas Ranger working with him helped. He kept thinking about his uncle and the sheriff's department. When the gunman from the airfield mentioned going back to the station, it didn't have to mean the police or sheriff's department. Could've been the news station. The gas station. Or a hundred other places. But his gut told him the place was law enforcement, since the man mentioned the sheriff.

His phone rang and Luke's name popped up on the screen. When he had talked to him fifteen minutes earlier, Luke said a vehicle had been found that fit the description of Sadie's car, but Rhett had chosen not to mention it to Brandi in case it didn't turn out to be her sister's. Normally he would use Bluetooth, but he was tempted to pull over and talk to the Ranger in private.

A hand reached out and touched his. Brandi's eyes pleaded. "I want to hear this. Please."

Against his better judgment, he answered the call. "This is Kincaid. You're on speaker and Brandi is with me."

That earned him a glare from his passenger, but he kept his attention on the call.

"Two things. First thing, it's confirmed. The car we found belonged to Sadie."

The air went from Rhett. Found her car but didn't find

her body? He glanced to Brandi and immediately saw the fear. "That's good news. How do you know it's Sadie's?"

"The car is registered in her name."

"Any sign of my sister?" Brandi spoke loudly toward the mic.

"No, ma'am. The car was empty."

Rhett scratched his head. He wished he could talk to Luke in private so he could prepare Brandi if there were any bad news. But it looked like it was too late for that.

"Where did you find the car?" she asked.

"Off Catfish Ridge Bridge west of town. Looks like it'd been dumped."

She looked at Rhett. "That bridge is only ten miles from Parker Airfield. She must've been run off the road after leaving the barracks."

"Could be." He turned his attention back to Luke. "Did you find anything else in the car?"

"Yeah. A diaper bag and John Graves's business card in the floorboard—the agent I just talked to you about."

"Interesting." Rhett glanced at Brandi. "That means the FBI must've been in contact with Sadie."

"I would think so. I tried to call the agent, but no answer."

"Good. Anything else? Have you heard back from Chasity about the bank withdrawal?"

"Nothing from Chasity. But yeah, the second thing, Deputy Norris's vitals are better. The doctor said if Norris continues to improve, he will take him out of his coma."

Brandi shot Rhett a smile. "That's good news. Did they say when?"

Luke's voice came across the speaker. "There's no way to know, but they're hoping in the next twenty-four hours. The sheriff's department put a security guard sta-

tioned outside his room. That's it so far. I'll let you know
if anything else turns up."

Brandi leaned over. "Thanks, Luke."

After he hit the end button, he searched Brandi's face.
She appeared deep in thought. Norris had a wife and two
teenage daughters, and Rhett could only imagine the
turmoil it put his family in. Even if the deputy pulled
through, what kind of rehab and limitations would he
endure?

"Why would the FBI contact Sadie and my grandmother, but not me?"

Rhett had wondered the same thing. "Maybe he just
hasn't gotten ahold of you yet." Her forehead wrinkled,
and he reached over and patted her hand. "You have nothing to hide. If the FBI is investigating, then we should
get to the bottom of the stolen money and attacks sooner
than later."

"I suppose you're right." She avoided eye contact and
looked out the passenger-side window. "I wonder if it
will put the deputy in danger since he could identify his
shooter."

"I was thinking the same thing."

"Great minds think alike."

"Yeah." Rhett enjoyed it when snippets of the old
Brandi resurfaced. The banter. Her dimply smile. "The
security guard should deter any trouble."

She nodded. "Yeah. I pray so, and I'm glad the department is taking the threat seriously."

He fixed his eyes on the road. It'd been good to see Estelle. He prayed that when this was all over Brandi would
be able to put the past behind her and reconnect with her
family. Her grandmother had worn a smile today like
always but had looked surprised to see Brandi. If only

Brandi could see what she had in front of her instead of what she was missing.

Rhett figured that was typical of most people.

What would he do with Brandi once the case—whether it turned out good or bad—was over? Two days ago, he hadn't expected to see his ex. When she'd walked out on their relationship, Brandi had not only shut the door but had locked it. Now that she was back, he didn't know what to think about that. He'd never wanted her to leave in the first place.

Like so many times, when he thought of Brandi leaving him, his mind returned to the time his dad had walked out. At nine, Rhett had sprinted out the screen door with tears running down his face and jumped off the wooden porch. He'd grabbed his dad's shirttail. "Please don't go, Daddy. Me and Pam will stay out of trouble and keep our room clean. Whatever you need. Just don't go."

His dad had pulled out of his grip and scoffed. "Don't cry like a girl, Rhett. You're as bad as your mama, with your beggin'. It's time you learn you don't get everything you want, boy."

His dad had stumbled to his old truck and never looked back.

You don't get everything you want. He stole a glance at Brandi. That much was true. He'd like to give their relationship another try, but what if she, too, walked away?

THIRTEEN

Brandi kept replaying in her mind all the information they'd gathered after the visit to her grandmother. What had triggered the FBI into investigating this case again? Did they have additional information?

She glanced at Rhett, glad he was beside her. It helped to bounce ideas off someone and brought back a lot of wonderful memories from before the tornado. He'd grown more serious than he used to be. Filled out a little more—all of it muscle. "Do you work out?"

The question slipped out before she could stop it.

His head jerked toward her, and a smile crept across his face. "When I have time. I like to run at home, either on the treadmill or on the road. Clears my head."

"Exercise seems to do that for a lot of people."

He quirked an eyebrow. "You still go to the gym?"

"Not anymore." She'd quit after Mulberry Gap turned against her family. She no longer got together with friends to work out at the gym or go for a healthy shake at the local nutrition store. All of her exercise was done solo. "I took up biking."

"Oh?" His eyes widened.

She didn't know why he sounded surprised. She loved to be outside. "I've always been an outdoor type of girl."

"I remember." His face went still. "It was one of the things I lo—enjoyed about you. You were never afraid to get dirty." A smile slipped across his lips. She thought he was through, but then he asked, "Do you remember when my uncle let us take his dirt bikes? We snuck into the old racetrack at night and rode over the mounds."

"How could I forget? You made me wipe out over that big hill. What did we call it? Mount Everest."

"Yeah." He smiled "But don't blame me that you wrecked. You gassed it and jumped Everest of your own free will. Went airborne and all."

Only two security lights had illuminated the track. She wouldn't have ridden so fast if she could've seen better. But why admit that to Rhett now? "You know how competitive I am, and you jumped first."

"So you *are* blaming me." He chuckled.

"Definitely." She tried to keep a straight face but failed. Riding bikes had been a blast.

"Remember the mud fight?" His perfect teeth showed through his smile.

"How could I forget?" After a short Texas downpour moved in, the track had become a mud bath before they could make it back to the pavement. Brandi had lost control and turned the bike over in the mud. She wasn't injured but got covered in muck from head to toe. When Rhett had laughed at her misery, she slung a mud ball at him, hitting him in the face. A massive fight ensued. It had ended with them both rolling around in filth and laughing hysterically.

Life had been good back then, with no worries. She

still had her family, the town respected them, and she had a handsome fiancé. "Those times were different."

"They sure were." His smile faded into somberness, and his eyes glistened. "I wouldn't trade them for anything in the world."

His words brought more joy than they ought. "Neither would I."

Boom!

An explosion had Brandi jerking forward.

"Get down. Get down." Rhett's hand pushed her head into the seat.

She unbuckled and sank to her knees on the floorboard. "What was that?"

"Someone shot out our back window."

Dizziness threatened as her legs went weak. Not again. "Who is it?"

"A black van. I haven't seen this one before." The truck swayed as Rhett tried to evade the shooter.

She sank even lower and retained her grip on the console and the seat. The truck lurched even faster. She kept her head down and couldn't see the speedometer, but it felt like they were flying.

"Get out of the way," Rhett mumbled. He swung to the left. Streetlights zoomed by as she glanced up and out of the window.

She moved to peek out, but Rhett commanded, "Stay low."

More bullets shot through the glass and ricocheted in the cab. Continuous blasts sounded like the Fourth of July.

"Hand me my gun."

Something warm ran down her back. She reached into

the console and handed him the weapon. Pain suddenly radiated across her shoulder.

She was shot!

No. No. No.

"Remember JV6BKE."

Wooziness overtook her and she crumbled on the floorboard, not able to comprehend Rhett's words. Tears blurred her vision in disbelief. *Please, God, don't let them kill Rhett. We're so close to finding the truth.*

Rhett's firing convinced whoever was in the van to slam on their brakes and pull behind him. A silver sedan lumbered ahead, and he swerved into the passing lane to go around. The van didn't let up its speed, but bumped the sedan's back bumper, sending the car spinning out of control and into the ditch.

His jaw tightened. The van could have easily avoided the hit. Why did they have to be dangerous to innocent bystanders? Anger gripped Rhett, but he sped down the highway trying to find a secure place to lose this guy.

He slowed for an upcoming curve and the van moved to the inside, down in the ditch and up beside them on the passenger side. "Stay down, Brandi."

Rhett pointed his Glock as the van pulled even. He fired his weapon at the same time as one of the men in the van did. There were at least two assailants in the other vehicle.

The black, boxy vehicle slowed and soon Rhett sped away. The police needed to get involved before innocent citizens suffered injuries. On a long stretch of highway, when the van was out of sight, he called into the Mulberry Gap Police Station to give them the vehicle's description and the license plate number.

"You can get up now." He glanced down at Brandi, glad she had remained quiet and out of the shooter's targets.

Her head lifted, but her face was pale and her eyes remained closed.

"What's wrong?" What was he thinking taking her out today? Brandi had always been tough, but only yesterday she had been in that frozen shelter.

Her jaw tightened, and she mumbled, "Nothing."

A dark place showed on her shirt. He reached down and his fingers came away wet. "You've been shot."

"I'm on fire."

His chest constricted with fear. He'd made a mistake. Brandi should've stayed with Pam until all this was over. Or he could've paid someone to help keep her safe while he worked the case. Anything but this. "I'll get you to the hospital."

He braked hard at the next right and swung onto a different highway. The van was no longer in sight, but he didn't know if they were still in pursuit. He slowed and moved to the side of the highway. From the back seat, he grabbed a towel, wadded it into a ball and gently placed it on her shoulder. "Keep this on it."

She struggled into the seat and placed the cloth over the wound.

He quickly called the hospital to notify them he was bringing in a gunshot victim. Then he called Luke Dryden and left a brief update on his voice mail. His foot hit the accelerator and they were back on the road. He was tempted to ask how badly the wound hurt, but he knew the answer. Shock or adrenaline could keep the pain at bay before the real pain settled in.

He glanced up at the ceiling. Why? Why hadn't he left her with Dryden for protection?

Because he wanted to be the one to protect her. Selfishness. Wanted to prove he was on her side, that she could depend on him. And now she'd been shot.

Brandi's eyes were closed, a frown firmly in place as she clamped her left arm with her right hand.

He murmured, "I'm sorry."

"It's not your fault." Her eyes flitted open.

"Sure, it is." Her words didn't ease his pain but made his guilt worsen. Of course, it was his fault. Texas Rangers were taught to protect, not put civilians in danger.

"Rhett, get me to the hospital. Please hurry."

"We're eight minutes away." Blood seeped through the towel. He leaned over and applied more pressure to the wound.

They pulled into the emergency drive-thru. Two men dressed in scrubs brought a stretcher out, loaded her up and disappeared behind sliding glass doors. Feeling like his world had left him standing alone, he got back in his truck and parked in the designated area. He called Luke back.

This time he answered, "This is Dryden."

"Brandi took a bullet. Just dropped her off at the ER and I'm on my way in. Did you learn anything?"

"We didn't find the van, but Mulberry police found one of its passengers."

"Yeah." He wasn't in the mood for guessing games.

"He's dead. Dumped on the side of Robin Road."

Rhett had figured the man was no longer of use. "Do you know his identity?"

"We think so. The officer at the scene thought the victim looked like Blaze Spalding, a twenty-year-old, slim and clean-cut guy attending classes at the local community college. The officer only remembers him because he pulled him over last week for speeding, but Spalding had been driving a vehicle registered to someone else. They're checking into it right now."

"Slim and clean-cut. That could've been the guy who stood over us in the shelter. Good job. Keep me posted. I'm going in the hospital to be with Brandi."

"Take care of the girl. I'll holler if the van turns up."

Rhett clicked off and hurried inside. He showed his credentials to the woman at the desk, who let him through. Brandi was hooked up to an IV and a nurse in scrubs worked beside her. The nurse looked up. "Are you Ranger Kincaid?"

"Yes, ma'am."

"We're prepping Miss Callahan for surgery to remove the bullet. She asked to see you."

His chest tightened as he walked over to Brandi. Her eyes drooped heavy with sedation, but her gaze met his. He clasped her hand without the IV to his chest. "I'll be right here when you get out."

A smile lifted the corner of her mouth. "Thanks."

"Okay, Mr. Kincaid, you need to move to the surgery waiting room through the double doors and to the right."

"Yes, ma'am." He placed a kiss on Brandi's hand before they wheeled her away. His throat grew tight as he watched her disappear behind closed doors. She'd come to him for help, and now she was headed into surgery with a bullet wound.

FOURTEEN

A soft hum of voices woke her. With a lot of effort, she shoved her eyes open to a dark and shadowed room. Grogginess filled her head as she struggled to get her bearings. A large shade covered a window to the right. Warmth radiated from her left.

She turned to see Rhett by her bedside, her hand encased in his.

His concerned brown eyes took her in, searching her face.

"Have you been here the entire time?" She cleared her throat from the dryness.

"Of course." He handed her a cup of ice and waited while she chewed a chip. "I wouldn't leave you at a time like this. How are you feeling?"

"Spacey." She blinked. "I'm trying to clear the cobwebs."

"Are you in pain?" His brow wrinkled. "I can get the nurse if you need more pain meds."

She shook her head and instantly regretted it, dizziness descending on her. Her head cleared seconds later. The last time she'd been in the hospital she had been twelve and had her tonsils removed. She'd awakened to her throat throbbing and her daddy sitting in the chair next to her bed.

A funny sensation fell over her. Even though she had taken a bullet in the shoulder, memories of a different time resurfaced. Daddy had always been her protector, and later, Rhett. Not that she was helpless, but someone had always been in her corner fighting alongside of her. She'd missed that feeling of being safeguarded.

What had Rhett asked? Pain meds. "I feel like I have cotton in my throat, but no pain right now."

"That's the way we want it." A tall man wearing a white coat whisked into the room, a nurse behind him. "I'm Dr. Lassiter."

Brandi attempted to focus, but her mind was too groggy. "I don't remember seeing you before."

He smiled. "I don't imagine you would. I talked to you for only a minute before you were under anesthesia. We removed a .22 caliber bullet from your left shoulder. Even though you'll be sore, no major arteries or veins were hit, and the muscle damage was minimal. But it will take time to heal."

She nodded and tried to concentrate on his words. The car chase. Getting shot in the shoulder. They had to put a stop to the madness and find Sadie. "How long will I have to stay?"

"We need to observe you for the next four to six hours. You weren't completely under and the bullet was not very deep. We need to be certain you're fully out of sedation and all your vitals are stable before you're released. I don't foresee any problems. I'll write you a prescription for pain to be used as needed and antibiotics to decrease the chance of infection. You'll be sore for the next couple of days. Take it easy and get plenty of rest. Need to see you for a checkup in my office in ten days."

"I will. Thank you."

"Try to stay away from gunfire, young lady. Not everyone is so blessed." He smiled. "Do you have questions?"

"No." She smiled. The doctor left the room. Was Sadie one of those who had escaped harm? Or had she come back into Brandi's life just to die now? Brandi could never accept that.

At least she would get released today. That was good because she couldn't stay in hospital while her sister was out there, maybe fighting for her life.

"Where's Levi?" She looked at Rhett.

"In the waiting room with Pam." He again touched her hand. "You're still a little pale, but you look much better. I want you to get rest so you're ready to go when you get released."

Brandi knew he was right, but she was prepared to go now.

"I'm going to make a few calls. Pam is outside the door if you need her."

"Is Levi doing all right?"

As if she heard, Pam stepped inside the room.

"Bandee."

She looked up to see Levi smiling. "Come in."

"Are you certain?" Pam asked. "You need your rest."

Brandi looked up at her nephew, the glow in his eyes. He was a handsome boy, dressed in the denim jacket, jeans and hiking boots Rhett had bought him. "I'd love to see him."

Rhett squeezed her hand. "I'm just a phone call away.

I'll be in the waiting room." He scrubbed Levi's head and bent down. "I'll be back, little buddy."

"'Kay." His little voice came out loud and clear.

Brandi smiled at the boy's reaction. Then Rhett leaned over and gave her a peck on the forehead.

She blinked. With an exhale of a deep breath, she watched him leave. He had always kissed her bye when he left while they were dating.

"He's still crazy about you, you know."

Brandi jerked at the words. "I don't know what you're talking about."

"Whatever." Pam laughed. "Sure, you do." She pulled up a chair and sat with Levi in her lap.

Brandi swallowed, trying to muster her courage for the topic. "We're too far past mending our relationship. Sure, it's good to see him again, and he's a nice guy. But Rhett and I both know where we stand."

"A nice guy." Pam laughed out loud this time. "If you say so."

Brandi's cheeks warmed, and she wondered if Pam noticed the flush. Probably.

Levi held out his hands. "Bandee."

Pam held him back. "She needs her rest."

"It's okay." Brandi adjusted the bed in an upright position. "Keep him on the right side and I should be fine."

Pam set him on the bed, and Brandi pulled him close under her arm. "Would you like to watch cartoons?"

He gave a big nod. "'Toons."

Brandi figured he was too young to understand the show but thought it would be a quiet distraction. She clicked on the television and found a kids' station. She turned the volume low.

"Do you need anything?" Pam asked. "Something to drink or eat? There's a vending machine down the hall."

"I'm not hungry and the water in the pitcher is fine. But you could buy something for Levi. I'm sure he'll be fine with me until you get back."

"I've got gummies in my purse." She pulled out a half-eaten package and offered them to Levi, who quickly snatched it.

Brandi settled back to the low hum of an older cartoon. It felt good to have people surrounding her again for a change. She'd missed Rhett and his family. And now little Levi. She had pulled away for so long she'd forgotten how helpful and fulfilling it could be to have people in your life. The last two years, she had felt a major void—like an empty glass that could never be filled. Regardless how much she exercised or what emergency calls she assisted with at work, life was meaningless.

Even going to worship services every week had suffered. As soon as the last amen was uttered, Brandi dashed for the back doors, hoping to escape anyone who wanted to visit with her. A quick bite grabbed through a drive-thru somewhere, and then she'd go home alone. A colossal difference from the large Sunday gatherings at Grandma's house with Rhett and the family after worship.

What would happen when the bad guys were caught? Rhett would go back to his Ranger life and she would go back to her tiny home on the other side of Mulberry Gap.

Sadness filled her. It was difficult to look forward to going back to a life of solitude. Hopefully, Sadie and Levi would be a part of her life. Her thoughts drifted to the simple things she used to enjoy. Rhett taking her fishing at the cabin. Grandma's famous chocolate over biscuits.

Her daddy humming gospel songs in the car on the way to worship services. Those were good times.

Sometime later, the buzzing of her phone woke her. The effects of the anesthesia still lingered. Brandi glanced around and found Levi still beside her, sound asleep. Pam wasn't in the room. Probably stepped out to use the restroom or get something to eat.

She tried to clear her mind as she picked up the cell. She recognized Shannon's number. Her boss had probably heard about the shooting and wanted to check on her. Or maybe Deputy Norris had regained consciousness. She whispered so as to not wake Levi. "Hello, boss."

"Brandi, I had to call you." Shannon talked fast. "I just heard on the police scanner there's a BOLO for you."

"What? I'm sitting in a hospital bed. I won't be difficult to find."

"Oh no," Shannon responded. "What happened?"

"I don't have time to explain." Evidently Shannon hadn't heard, since Rhett didn't call it in. Hospital personnel were required to report gunshot wounds, so it wouldn't be long before someone notified law enforcement. "What is the BOLO for?"

"A neighbor of yours called the police because her dog brought home a man's shoe with blood on it. The police were called, and they found an FBI agent dead in your storage building."

"What?" Brandi sucked in her breath. "This can't be happening. They're setting me up. I haven't seen or talked to anyone from the FBI. I've got to go." She clicked off and immediately dialed Rhett's number. As the phone rang, she climbed out of bed, careful not to wake Levi. The call went to voice mail.

"Rhett, it's me. I need help now. Please call me."

With her heart racing, she moved across the room and found her clothes in a plastic bag. She hurriedly changed, even though weakness made her uncoordinated, and a couple of times she had to use the wall for support.

"What are you doing?" Pam stood in the door with a steaming foam cup in her hand.

"I've got to get out of here." She didn't want to tell Pam the police had a BOLO out on her in case they questioned Rhett's sister. Didn't want to put Pam in a position to lie. "If Rhett calls, tell him he needs to call me pronto. Oh no, I don't have a car." She looked at Pam. "Can I use yours?"

"Sure." Her eyes widened before she dug into her purse and handed her the keys. "I'm parked in the south parking lot."

Brandi secured her purse and was walking out the door when she heard Levi stir.

"Bandee gone?"

Her heart stopped. "I'll be back. Okay? Brandi will be back."

Concern stretched across his forehead as he slowly nodded. "'Kay. Bandee back."

As she rushed out the door, she prayed it wasn't a lie. If Sadie didn't make it back in his life, Brandi needed to be there for him. She couldn't do that from jail.

The elevator doors opened and a Mulberry Gap police officer stepped out.

This can't be happening. She stepped back into the room, allowing the door to close.

Pam stepped up behind her and peeked into the hallway. Her eyes cut to Brandi. "Give me a second and then I want you to go."

Brandi nodded.

Pam grabbed Levi, stepped out the door and hurried down the hall. "Excuse me, officer. I'm on the Mulberry Gap Citizens Action Committee and I have a couple of questions."

As soon as the officer's back was turned, Brandi bolted from the room, around the right side of the nurses' station and down the hallway to the stairwell. The fast movement caused her head to spin, but she couldn't afford to slow down. As she slipped through the door, she fell into a wall before regaining her balance. She had to find Rhett before the law found her.

Rhett checked his GPS again. He was still over ten minutes away from the homeless shelter in Cotton Mill County. Dryden had called forty-five minutes ago and asked Rhett to meet him. He'd found a woman who recognized Sadie's picture at this shelter.

Rhett didn't have all the details, but from what he could make out, the woman had met Sadie in a shelter in Painted Rock over a year ago. The town was about four hours away. The woman said Sadie had a newborn boy with her.

Brandi had been asleep with Levi in the hospital bed, and Pam was working on her iPad when he left the room. The hospital was the safest place to leave Brandi while he investigated the lead. He didn't have the heart to wake her to discuss the possible development. Not that he had much choice. He didn't have intentions of placing her in danger anymore. Besides, if this turned out to be a dead end, he didn't want her hopes squashed. He prayed this woman wasn't pulling their legs about knowing Sadie in the hope of monetary gain.

His truck bounced over the crumbling pavement as he

pulled into the facility at the end of the street. A bread store sat across from the shelter and a small clapboard church building on the other. He went to put his phone on vibrate and noticed there were no bars—no signal. This shouldn't take long.

He strode up the sidewalk and opened the steel door.

The sound of mumbled voices and a crying baby echoed through the halls.

A lone artificial Christmas tree, sparsely decorated with what appeared to be homemade decorations of popcorn string and paper cut-out angels, cowered in the far corner. He assumed the angels were a wish list for its residents. No presents sat under the tree, just a tattered white sheet of batting.

He swallowed down his emotions. If Uncle Duke and Aunt Lauren hadn't stepped in, he and his sister could have very well ended up in a shelter like this with his mom.

Luke Dryden stepped out of a room and motioned for him. "This way."

Rhett strode down the hall, shoving the memories to the back of his mind. He needed to find Sadie, not get distracted with his past. When he walked into the room, a slender woman with red hair and surprisingly bright eyes sat in an old office chair with ripped fabric. She couldn't have been older than thirty. The coffee mug in her hand read I Only Speak to My Dog before Coffee. She glanced up at him.

"Rhett, this is Stormy Fowler." Luke turned to her. "Stormy, this is my partner, Ranger Rhett Kincaid."

Stormy scrutinized him behind sharp green eyes. He felt ashamed for expecting someone who looked like a drug user.

"Glad to meet you, Ranger Kincaid." She shifted in her chair and sat straight. "But I know you didn't come to meet the lovely residents at Cotton Mill County Homeless Shelter."

"No, ma'am." He smiled.

At the polite address, she gave him a second look.

Luke shoved a photograph of Sadie on the desk toward Stormy. "Tell him what you told me, please." Luke was tall and slim, with a contagious smile. Most women probably found him attractive. There was no one Rhett would rather have at his side when interviewing witnesses. Luke's easygoing manner encouraged people to relax, and no doubt Stormy might've never opened up without him there.

"I know this woman." She pointed a finger at the picture. "She went by the name Cindy McGowen, though. We met over in Painted Rock about a year ago. Had an infant with her. Don't recall the name."

Rhett's first instinct said the woman was on the up-and-up, but it was important they find out if it was indeed Sadie whom she'd met. "Was the baby a boy or girl?"

Stormy Fowler sipped her coffee. "A boy. Precious thing. Looked a lot like his daddy. Or at least I presume the guy was his daddy."

"Do you know the man's name?"

She shook her head. "Oh, he didn't talk to us 'shelter losers.' He made that clear." She raised an eyebrow and marked Rhett with a glare like she hadn't been happy with the phrase. "And even though me and the dad weren't introduced, Cindy droned on about the father occasionally when she thought no one was listening. One time she was roaring mad that the daddy hadn't sent money, and she ranted about him being the sheriff's son. When I asked why she didn't simply go home, Cindy claimed she couldn't because everyone believed she was dead. I told her they would figure it out when she waltzed in and joined them for Thanksgiving turkey." Stormy grinned, and then the delight faded. "The humor seemed to be lost on Cindy."

No, Sadie probably wouldn't think that was funny. "Did she say why they thought she was dead?"

Stormy looked him and Luke over. "Is she in trouble? How do I know you're not planning to arrest her?"

"You don't," Rhett said. "But that's not in my plans. However, if she is guilty of a crime, that *could* happen. Sadie's sister is searching for her." He didn't know how much to tell this woman, but he thought sharing the information was better than worrying if Stormy would warn Sadie. "Brandi, Sadie's sister, is an emergency dispatcher. Sadie called 911 two mornings ago, and Brandi took the call. The line disconnected before Sadie could tell her what was wrong. Sadie only got in something about her grandparents' farm. When Brandi arrived a few minutes later, she found a toddler abandoned in the old barn. Brandi is desperately trying to find his mother."

"Levi?"

Neither Rhett nor Luke had mentioned his name. A glance to Luke said he'd noticed the slipup, as well. "That's his name."

Rhett pulled up a photograph of Wes on his phone and held it out to her.

"That's him. Levi's daddy." Stormy mumbled a couple of choice names for Rhett's cousin. "That was the man who visited Cindy, uh, Sadie at the shelter. He wasn't none too happy she was there, either. Called her useless and said she wasn't good enough to be a mama to his child. Sadie argued that his parents had money and pleaded she could get a better job if they could help her get a car and she didn't have to wait on the public transportation van. She promised to pay them back when she had the money. The jerk just laughed at her and told her she was an embarrassment. The icing on the cake was when he told her he'd be back for the boy." Stormy shoved Rhett's phone back to him. "That's when Sadie left. Snuck out in the middle of the night."

"Did you try to get in touch with her?"

"Nope." Stormy shook her head. "If someone doesn't want to be found, I leave 'em alone. People's secrets are none of my business."

Rhett had the feeling there was much more to Stormy's life story, but he didn't pry. He would like to come back sometime to see if she needed assistance. "You've been a big help. If you remember anything more or hear from Sadie, please call me."

Stormy's gaze went from Luke back to Rhett again, like she was debating saying something. "You really do care about her?"

"Yes, I do." Rhett answered too quickly and in the singular, eliciting a second glance.

As if Luke sensed the distraction, he said, "Ma'am, Rhett told you the truth. Sadie's sister has the boy, and we're afraid she is in trouble. Brandi is in the hospital right now with a gunshot wound. We have no tricks. No good cop, bad cop games. We just need to find Sadie."

Stormy glanced back at the open door, presumably to make sure no one was listening. She bent forward and whispered, "Cindy—I mean Sadie—contacted me a couple of months ago. She planned to talk to the FBI. Something about coming clean. Long ago, Sadie quit doing drugs even though her loser boyfriend kept pushing them toward her, so I don't think it meant she was coming clean from drugs. Sadie was a private person, and I didn't meddle. But I liked her. A good kid. You know?"

Rhett leaned closer and made direct eye contact. "Did Sadie say what she wanted to talk to the agent about?"

Stormy shook her head. "Nothing besides coming clean."

Sadie was a kid when he and Brandi dated. A typical teenager, but a little promiscuous. Rhett merely nodded.

"Sadie mentioned a sister a couple of times. Since she rarely talked about anyone from her past, I knew the sister and her must've been close."

"Brandi would be happy to know that."

"Will you let me know if you hear from her?" Concern etched across her face. "I've been worried ever since she called about the FBI agent."

"Is there anything else?"

She shook her head.

"Thank you, Stormy. If you remember something, will you give us a call?"

She nodded. "I will."

He and Luke exchanged glances, indicating they had no more questions.

Luke reached into his wallet and pulled out a hundred-dollar bill.

Stormy held up her hand. "Put that away. I don't take money for helping a friend."

Both the Rangers tipped their hats to her and left the room. He and Luke met outside the shelter.

Luke said, "I like her."

"Yeah. She seemed trustworthy." Rhett glanced back at the building, knowing a lot of women and children stayed there. They put the children's names on the angel tree in businesses across town and he'd bought a couple of gifts every year, but this year he would inquire what else the shelter needed.

Rhett gave Luke a slap on the back as he did so often when greeting him or saying goodbye. "Thanks for your help. I need to get back to the hospital and check on Brandi. She should be released soon."

"I'll head back to Mulberry Gap, too. If Sadie is the one who initiated contact with the FBI, they may know more about this case than we do. I'll make some calls to see what I can learn."

"That explains why Agent John Graves was interviewing Brandi's grandmother. You still haven't gotten ahold of him?"

"No, I left a couple of messages on his voice mail."

"Talk to you later." As Rhett strode to his truck, he glanced at his phone. Four missed calls and one voice mail from Brandi.

His chest tightened, making it difficult to breathe. A sour taste developed in his mouth. Four calls meant bad news. Brandi wasn't one to keep on calling back once she left a message.

When he tried to call her back, he noticed again he had no bars.

Maybe she was being released early from the hospital. But his gut said no. Pam was there to take her home, so he doubted that was why she called.

Brandi had faced too many dangerous situations the last two days. Something told Rhett things were about to get much worse and he had to get back. Now.

FIFTEEN

Brandi hadn't driven a stick shift since she was a teen-ager and Daddy had her drive the old grain truck back and forth to the pasture during harvest. Pam's little red Miata was a manual, and Brandi's feet struggled clumsily to find the correct pedal. Definitely not like riding a bike. She approached a stop sign in the parking lot, and the car didn't slow as her foot hit the clutch. Her heart raced. At the last second, she panicked, and her left foot found the brake, slinging her forward.

No wonder automobile companies had practically quit making manuals. She exhaled a breath when the car finally made it to the street.

She looked around, half expecting to see multiple police cars surround the little car. But she eased into traffic, driving the speed limit so as to not draw attention.

Deputy Norris had been shot in her presence and now this. The feeling she had become a criminal flowed through her. It was silly, of course, because she knew nothing of the agent found at her house. Why would he be in her storage shed? Or had someone moved his body after they killed him?

She was being set up.

Had to be. Her nerves were frayed as she turned onto the main highway. A police cruiser sat on the corner of a convenience store parking lot across the street. Brandi kept her eyes glued straight ahead, but after she passed, a check to her rearview mirror showed the vehicle hadn't moved. Her breath whooshed out of her again.

Another call to Rhett's cell went to voice mail. "Come on, Rhett," she said. "Please answer the phone. It's important. I need you to call me back."

Where was he? Was he in trouble?

She refrained from leaving details in case something had happened to him and his cell had wound up in the wrong hands. She had to get out of town. Maybe back to the cabin.

Her shoulder slightly throbbed even though she hadn't been off the pain meds since her surgery. As she neared the edge of town, she picked up speed. No one should be looking for a red Miata. She clutched the steering wheel. The hunting cabin was no good. What if the sheriff remembered the place? She couldn't worry about where to go; she just had to get far away from Mulberry Gap.

Her cell rang, making her jump. Rhett's number. *Finally.* "Where have you been?"

"Luke got a call from a woman who recognized Sadie. I called Pam and left a message on her phone."

"I'm being set up. Shannon called me. That FBI agent showed up dead in my storage shed." Brandi topped the hill going sixty-five, glad to finally be out of town and headed west. "Now's there a BOLO on me. I'm not going to jail."

"Where are you? Brandi, I won't let anything happen to you."

A siren blasted from behind her, making her jump. An

unmarked deputy's car pulled in behind her. She glanced around, searching for an exit. "Oh no."

Rhett asked, "What is it?"

"A deputy's car. He's trying to pull me over."

"Don't try to outrun him. If there's a BOLO out on you, he's just doing his job."

"No. I'm in Pam's car. How did he recognize me? They know my every move. I'm being framed for murder." She couldn't hold back the panic from her voice, and the siren and flashing lights only made it worse. "Someone in law enforcement has been behind the whole thing. Or Phil is in cahoots with someone on the force. As soon as I'm behind bars, they'll plant more evidence."

"Can you identify the deputy?"

Her hands shook on the steering wheel, and she slowed to get a better look. "Deputy Coble."

"Hasn't he always been fair to you?"

"Yes."

"What's your location?"

She looked to the pasture to the right and recognized the large cattle pens. "Farm-to-market road 62, near the Stover place."

"Okay. I know where that's at. I'm an hour away. Pull over and do what Coble asks, except don't answer any questions. Politely tell him you'd like to talk to a lawyer. If he arrests you, don't say anything. Nothing. I'll be there as fast as I can."

Instinct told her to make a run for it. "Who will find Sadie?"

"I will. I promise, I won't quit searching until we find her."

"Okay." Her voice shook.

"Brandi, don't try to outrun the deputy."

Wouldn't her chances be better if she could get away? Maybe she could floor it when the deputy was almost to her door.

"Brandi?"

She rubbed her hand across her face. "I won't run."

"Okay. We'll get through this together." Rhett's voice trailed off.

She hung up and placed her cell in the passenger seat. Coble was so close to her bumper she couldn't see the lights in his grill. She gave the wheel a last good squeeze and let off the accelerator and moved onto the shoulder of the highway.

Breathe, just breathe. *Please, Lord, don't let him arrest me.*

The deputy turned off his siren but left the lights swirling. She grabbed her license from her purse and got ready. Comply. Be reasonable. Coble had known her family for years.

As he walked up, she rolled down her window. When she turned, a gun was pointed in her face.

"Get your hands on the steering wheel."

"It's just my driver's license." She held the plastic in full view and did as he asked. "I have nothing else in my hand."

He opened her door. "Get out and keep your hands in the air."

"Yes, sir. I'm unarmed." Couldn't he simply ask for her to go to the station instead of making a big production? He could see she had no weapon. Her knees shook as she attempted to climb out of the tiny car while keeping her hands in the air. Her legs shook so badly she stumbled forward and fell into the door, before regaining her balance.

When her gaze met his, fury stared back. He jerked her injured arm close, sending sharp pangs of pain down her shoulder. She cried out. Cold metal stabbed her temple as Coble shoved his gun into her.

Please, don't let the gun go off.

"Get in my car," he growled.

This wasn't a normal arrest. Deputy Coble opened his back door and shoved her in. Her nose struck the back of the driver's seat before ricocheting back and causing her shoulder to slam into the back seat. She dropped into the floorboard. Shock waves of pain radiated through her.

What was wrong with the deputy?

Coble got in and took off at high speed away from Mulberry Gap.

Brandi blinked, trying to clear her mind as she swallowed down terror. At least Rhett knew who had pulled her over and where. But where was Coble taking her? Rhett had instructed her not to answer questions but had said nothing about asking them. "Where are we going? Are you arresting me?"

"Don't worry about it, Snookums. You'll figure it out soon enough."

Snookums? What was wrong with the man? He had always been friendly to her, even when the rest of the sheriff's department treated her like a suspect. Careful not to bump her shoulder, she crawled into the seat directly behind him. Even though the deputy hadn't bothered to handcuff her, a metal panel separated her from Coble, making overpowering him an impossibility. The car glided across the pavement like a land cruiser at a ridiculous rate of speed.

Instinctively, she snapped on her seat belt. She had to think. They were moving much too fast for Rhett to make it back in time to help her. She'd have to escape on her own.

A glance to the floorboard showed nothing she could use for a weapon. Not that she expected to find anything, but she couldn't wait to see what Coble had planned before she made a move. Would she be better off jumping out of the vehicle? Maybe. As a last resort.

Coble had always been friendly. Approximately sixty years old and nearing retirement. She knew little about his personal life but thought he had a wife and son. A family man. Or maybe he and his wife were divorced— she couldn't remember. "I don't know what you believe I've done, but I'm innocent. I didn't steal the tornado fund, and neither did my father." Rhett had said not to talk, but Rhett hadn't foreseen Coble's attack. Desperate situations called for desperate measures. "I didn't shoot Deputy Norris. I know you don't believe me, but a gunman shot him."

Coble laid his head back and laughed. "You seriously don't know what any of this is about. Do you? Poor little Miss Callahan. Raised by a rich banker who had the power to shatter people's lives and dreams."

Rich banker? Her dad had been a vice-president of the small local bank and had made a decent living, but they were far away from being rich. Why all the animosity toward her dad? "You knew my dad. He was a good man. Surely you don't believe he took the money?"

"He sure did," Coble spat. "Stole livelihoods from his customers every day!"

Every day? What did that mean? Coble thought her dad stole from customers. That made no sense.

"Keep trying to get that pretty brain of yours to work. You should be able to figure it out. Must be nice to be the daughter of a very important man. So was Sadie, but of course, she hung out with the wrong people." He snorted. "Don't you think she and the sheriff's son made the perfect couple? Two offspring of powerful men who used their position to hurt others."

Coble turned onto a rock road on the far southwest side of the county. She had never been out this way, but she needed to escape before they made it further onto the unbeaten path. The man made no sense, but she kept her mouth shut.

Rhett wouldn't be able to find her.

A curve appeared up ahead. Brandi would not get a better chance.

She had to jump.

Silently, she unbuckled her seat belt and got ready. *Please don't be one of those vehicles that have those back doors that can't open from the inside.* As Coble slowed for the turn, she took a deep breath and pulled on the handle. She thrust the door open.

Gravel flashed as the ground whizzed by, and she leaped.

Bam. She hit the ditch, the anguish sharp and shocking. The landing no doubt caused damage, but she didn't have time to consider her injuries.

The deputy's cruiser slid on the gravel.

She didn't look back. A barbwire fence intertwined with trees stood between her and a herd of Black Angus cows grazing. She sprinted through the ditch to gain distance. After a few steps, a thinning of the trees emerged, and she climbed through the fence, catching her jeans leg on a barb.

"Stop!"

She heard a loud explosion and the whiz of a bullet into a nearby limb.

With a powerful jerk, she was free and tearing across the pasture. The cows scattered ahead of her.

Her chest squeezed as her breath came in painful bursts. Coble was older and out of shape. Running was her greatest chance of escape. Holes from hoofprints made sprinting problematic, but she had no choice. Her right foot hit a hole, and thanks to the blind spot in her eye, she didn't see a thornbush and trampled over it. Her knee gave way, causing her to stumble. She regained her balance and continued running.

"Stop, Callahan. I'll kill you." His angry voice echoed across the field. Another blast and a bullet whizzed past her ear. "I'll kill Sadie. So help me, she'll die a painful death."

Brandi fell in the tall grass, tears of frustration flowing freely.

Heavy panting as Coble struggled for breath and then his black shoes appeared in front of her. "You're going to pay for running, Callahan."

Roughly, he jerked her to her feet and dug his fingers into her bicep.

"Ow. Ow." She grimaced and went to her tiptoes as she tried to ease the pain. She was not above begging. "I was shot in my shoulder today. Please be careful."

"I know you were shot," he spat, and didn't ease his viselike grip. "Who do you think ordered the attack on you and your sister?"

Why? "What did we ever do to you? Don't you think if I'm going to die, I should at least know why?"

Once they were back in the cruiser—her again in the back seat—they ate up the ground in the opposite direction of the main highway. A metal sign riddled with bullet holes contained a faded red arrow and read Morrison Junkyard ½ Mile. A junkyard? The deputy could shoot and bury her in a trash heap. Her body might never be found.

"Your daddy's death wasn't planned, but I wasn't upset when I heard about it."

The air was sucked from Brandi's lungs. She had known he hadn't taken his own life.

"Wes and your sister were caught stealing the tornado fund on your dad's home computer." A strange smiled formed on Coble, and he shook his head. "The funny part is the sheriff helped his son stage the suicide at the barn. Don't you get it yet, Callahan? You and your sister will never survive. I can't let you. It was your dad's and the sheriff's fault my son died in prison. Your well-to-do daddy denied me a loan to help pay for a good defense lawyer instead of that ignorant novice the court appointed. Jordan said I didn't have the *credit*. Well, la-di-da." His voice became even more shrill. "If the sheriff had given my boy another chance like he did his own scumbag offspring instead of arresting him, no one would've gotten hurt. If he had given Charlie half the help he gave Wes, my son would've never gone to prison."

Charlie Coble. Brandi barely recalled the guy. All she could remember was a guy with long hair, covered in tattoos. Seemed like he was sent to alternative school for some reason.

The deputy spat. "If that wasn't enough, your daddy denied me financial assistance after I lost my barn in the tornado! Seriously, everyone who lost property was supposed to get their share." He poked himself in the chest and smiled. "I finally got my money with Wes and

Sadie's help. Easy when the sheriff's son has a heap of gambling debts. A boy will pretty much do anything to keep his daddy from learning the truth."

She did remember her dad saying a few townspeople were upset their money was denied because the damage had to be a dwelling where they lived, not other outbuildings. But her father had never mentioned anyone by name.

"Jordan Callahan and Sheriff Kincaid thought they ran this town, not caring who got hurt. Well, it's time they learn their lesson." He chuckled. "Wait, your daddy already learned his."

Brandi's stomach tied into knots. She was afraid to say anything for fear Coble would go berserk. All this—her father's death, the stolen money and Sadie's disappearance—was because of the deputy's revenge?

A few minutes later, he whipped in and flew up the long drive and then slammed on the brakes, flinging her forward.

A pasture with a mixture of old cars, metals beams and parts, a railroad car and a rusted crane lay out in front of them.

With no weapons available, she reached down and slid off her running shoe. She must fight. Never give up. If Sadie were here, she'd find her.

"Time to rumble." He bent to let her out of the car, with his weapon in his other hand. She sprang into action and slammed against the door. Temporarily catching him off guard, she reared back with her shoe and swung hard at his face. Perfect connection. The audible slap was followed by his curse.

Using her good arm like an offensive lineman, she shoved past him, ready to run for her life.

Gunfire went off. "I'll shoot you in the back if I must, Jordan Callahan's daughter."

Brandi hesitated—wanting to run but didn't doubt he'd shoot her in the back. Her arms dropped to her side.

"You're going to pay for that." He rubbed his hand across his face before he grabbed her by the arm and jerked her toward him, her body slamming against his. "Don't try that again or I'll make certain you die a torturous death."

She stumbled across the overgrown yard. How would Rhett find her? What about Sadie? Had Coble already killed her?

After getting this close, she would never see her family and Rhett again. Even her mom had lost so much, but Brandi had been so absorbed with hurt and bitterness she couldn't see what she still had.

She should've remained close to family.

Now she might never have the chance. If only Rhett were here. But he'd never be able to find her in time. Even as the thoughts raced through her mind, she sought a way of escape.

After Rhett spotted his sister's empty red Miata on the side of the highway, he tried multiple times to get Brandi on the phone again, but no answer. Maybe Coble had arrested her. Out of everyone on the force, he seemed the most levelheaded when it came to Brandi. He'd been the most helpful in trying to find Sadie and hadn't spouted smart remarks about the Callahans.

Or had it been a ruse? Could Coble have stayed involved to steer them away from finding Sadie?

He pushed in his uncle's number.

"Don't be trying to hide her, boy."

Rhett let the boy comment slide. "Did you send Coble to arrest Brandi?"

"What? No. There's a BOLO out for her. We need to bring her in for questioning in the killing of an FBI agent. The feds will be swarming this town. She's in big trouble this time and neither you nor I can protect her."

"Uncle, listen. I don't have time to argue. Deputy Coble pulled Brandi over outside of Mulberry Gap. Has he checked in?"

"No. He's off today."

"If he has Brandi, where would he take her?"

"I have no idea."

Frustration ate at Rhett, making his stomach roll. He didn't have time for this. "I'll talk to you soon." He hung up and called Dryden. He relayed everything he knew, and Luke agreed to meet him at the farm.

Luke added, "I was going to call you anyway. I just heard Deputy Norris is awake and talking."

"Anything about his shooter?"

"Yeah. A guy by the name of Joe Dudley. Get this, he's supposedly a cousin of Deputy Coble. Norris hasn't said who sent him to the farm or why."

"Joe. He was one of the men at the airfield. Thanks. See you in a bit." A slow chill came over Rhett. There was no way to know who or how many people were involved, but Coble was at the top of the list. If Coble sent Norris to the farm that morning, why? To kill Brandi. Why did Dudley shoot Norris? A command by Coble or a wrong-place-at-the-wrong-time situation?

Even if Coble was behind the attacks, he'd never take Brandi to the farm.

He never should've told her to pull over for Coble, but the thought of running from law enforcement hadn't seemed like a viable option. Brandi had mentioned numerous times how she didn't trust the Jarvis County Sheriff Department and that they might be involved in her father's death and Sadie's disappearance. He hadn't believed it.

Was his uncle involved, too? It hurt his heart to believe someone he cared so deeply for could hurt another family. Especially someone who had promised to uphold the law and protect others.

About ten miles away from the farm, his phone rang again. Aunt Lauren.

"This is Rhett."

"Rhett, it's me," she whispered. "Don't tell your uncle I called, but I overheard him talking and thought you needed to know."

"Go ahead." His aunt cared a lot for him, and when he was a child, she would pull him aside to give him advice to keep him out of trouble. She respected her husband but disagreed with him at times.

"Duke's phone has been ringing off the hook. I'm worried. He said something about Wes, Deputy Coble and the junkyard. And then he mentioned…" She went silent.

"I'm listening."

"Sorry, your uncle walked through the room." Her whisper became even quieter. "Your uncle mentioned Brandi. I'm worried about you two. I hope I did right by telling you."

"Thank you. And you did right." He hung up. There were a couple of junkyards in the county, but Morrison was west of Mulberry Gap, closer to where she'd been pulled over. He called Luke as he turned his truck around. He filled his partner in on the conversation.

"How do you want to handle this?"

"Coble is definitely in on this, but I don't know about my uncle."

"I agree. Rhett, I will be glad to handle your uncle. I know what he means to you."

Memories of the first night he stayed in his aunt and uncle's house flitted through his mind. Rhett had been angry with his father. Even though he tried to hide the tears, his aunt and uncle were certain to have noticed his red eyes. His aunt had made a bed on the couch in the living room.

After his aunt and cousins had gone to bed, Uncle Duke had come and sat beside him. His uncle had put his arm around him and said, "I know things have been tough lately, boy. You are always welcome in our home. If you ever need to talk, I'll be here." That was all he'd said. Uncle Duke never bad-mouthed his own brother or Rhett's mom, but had just stepped in and been a man Rhett could look up to.

"No, I can do my job." Rhett cleared his throat from emotion. "I will keep an open mind and not jump to conclusions." At least he hoped he could. Luke and he continued to discuss options of how they needed to approach the situation, and then Luke agreed to update Lieutenant Adcock on recent developments. They clicked off.

Please, Lord, protect Brandi until I get there.

SIXTEEN

Brandi neared panic mode by the time Coble dragged her across the yard to the leaning rusty railroad car. She didn't see any vehicles other than the demolished ones in the dumping ground. But there were so many hiding places—a dozen could be a hidden among the rubbish.

Pieces of metal lay scattered everywhere and any one of them would make an excellent weapon if she could get free from the deputy's grasp. As if he read her mind, his grip on her bicep intensified, and he shoved her around the corner of the railroad car.

Brandi gasped as pain shot through her.

Her eyes lit on a figure in the corner.

Sadie sat huddled with a filthy blanket.

Her sister was alive! Brandi's mouth dropped open and she almost cried with relief. But then she got a good look at her sister. *No.*

Her younger sister's face was withdrawn and sickly. Dried blood was smeared across her forehead. An older gunman, thick and burly, stood close, with a gun jabbed in her sister's side. He was the man who'd attacked her at the farm and shot Deputy Norris. Brandi jerked against Coble's grip. "What did you do to her?"

"Simmer down, Callahan, if you want your sister to live another minute."

Fury and despair clawed at Brandi's soul. How could a person do this to another human being? Deputy Coble had been the one officer who'd been supportive. It was all a sham.

Sadie's gaze connected with hers. "Brandi?" Her voice came out so feeble Brandi could barely make out the word. "Where's my baby?"

"Levi's safe." Brandi's body throbbed with tension. She wanted to take on her sister's despair. She'd gladly accept any pain Coble wanted to inflict if he'd just leave Sadie alone.

"The boy won't be for long," Coble taunted.

Brandi clenched her jaw. "You'll never get away with this! Rhett will come after you. The town of Mulberry Gap will never stand for it." To her surprise, Brandi believed the words as she said them aloud.

"I'm planning on your boyfriend coming for you, Snookums. I wouldn't have it any other way." His sly smile sent chills down her spine. Coble was enjoying his moment in the spotlight.

"I don't get it. Why did you come after me? I didn't even know Sadie contacted the FBI." She had to stall him until Rhett arrived. *If* Rhett could find her.

Sadie sagged against the side of the railroad car. Her sunken eyes told Brandi more was wrong with her sister than what Coble and the gunman had done to her. Was she on drugs? Hopefully not, but that would explain why she hadn't come home for two years.

"I had to assume your sister told you I planned and paid Wes to steal the tornado fund when she called. But it doesn't matter. It's not a good feeling to have the people you love murdered." Coble said mockingly.

"My family never murdered anybody. I'm sorry about your son, but Charlie needed help."

Coble's face fumed red. "Your dad and the sheriff are as guilty as if they wielded the knife to my boy in that prison cell. They don't care about the little guy. I figure if the law won't prosecute them, I will."

"Put the weapon down, Deputy Dan Coble."

The deputy spun at the sound of Rhett's voice with his gun still in his grasp. Then Coble said to his partner, "Where is Davin?"

The big man shrugged. "I don't know."

Flooded with relief, Brandi found her knees buckling. She fought to keep her balance as she tried to move away from Coble. When he reached for her, she spun out from his grip and fled to Rhett.

"Brandi, down," Rhett shouted.

She dropped to her knees and gunfire exploded.

Coble fell to the dirt, his gun hand outstretched. A bloodstain spread over his shirt as he clutched his chest. "Shoot Sadie. Kill the girl."

The big man turned to her sister, but Luke Dryden stepped from behind the car, his gun aimed. "Don't do it, Dudley."

Fury registered on Coble's face even as sweat beaded across his forehead and blood drained from his face. His voice was weak. "Get Sadie!"

Luke pointed his weapon, and in a calm voice said, "Joe Dudley, put your weapon down. Norris has already identified you as his shooter."

The burly man's gaze darted around as he tried to find an escape.

"Now." Luke's finger tightened on the trigger.

Dudley's nostrils flared and his loud breathing displayed his rage, but he did as he was told.

Brandi climbed to her feet.

With his weapon still in hand, Rhett approached Coble and kicked his gun out of reach.

"You're not getting away, Kincaid." The deputy slowly smiled, his wild eyes trained on Rhett. "There are too many people on my side."

With Luke handcuffing Dudley and Rhett handling Coble, Brandi moved beside Sadie and put her arm protectively around her shoulder. "I've got you. Let's get you out of here, somewhere safe."

"I'm so sorry," Sadie said with desperation in her voice. "This is all my fault."

"Shh." Brandi helped her to her feet and talked quietly. "We'll discuss this later."

"You're bleeding." Shock registered on Sadie's face.

"I'm all right. We've got to move." Brandi felt moisture through her shirt but couldn't worry about the injury now. She had to get Sadie far away from danger. He'd mentioned other people being on his side. Who did he mean?

Sadie's face wrinkled into a frown. "I'm so sorry for everything. Where is Levi?"

"He's safe with Pam Kincaid."

"Rhett's sister? I remember her. But's Levi's okay? He didn't get too cold in the barn?"

"No. He was safe." Afraid her sister would break down and make it more difficult to get her to safety, Brandi ignored her babblings and pulled her around the corner of the railroad car. "Come on. You're almost home."

"No, she's not."

Brandi jerked at the sound of the familiar voice and her heart sank.

Rhett put pressure on Coble's wound, trying to stop the bleeding. But even as he tried, he knew it was too late. The deputy was dead.

In full view of everyone, the sheriff pulled up. At least his uncle wasn't trying to sneak up. Rhett stood and waited while the sheriff approached, but he kept his weapon ready.

"What's going on?" his uncle asked.

"Deputy Coble abducted Brandi and his gunman was holding Sadie Callahan hostage here at the junkyard. When he tried to shoot her, I took him out."

Kincaid glanced at his deputy on the ground and then to Joe Dudley. Rhett couldn't help but think something was wrong. He watched to make certain his uncle didn't go for his gun.

The sheriff swiped his forehead with the back of his hand. "We need to sort this out."

"I agree," Rhett said. "But I'm not letting anyone go until there's been an investigation. There's a murdered FBI agent, and Deputy Norris named Dudley here as his shooter. We still don't know where the stolen money is or who killed Jordan Callahan. Yes, we don't believe the banker committed suicide." Rhett's gaze met his uncle's, trying to gauge his reaction.

His uncle's shoulders sagged.

"Why don't you tell him, Sheriff?" Dudley spouted.

Rhett continued, "We will get to the bottom of this. The FBI and the Texas Rangers are already involved." No matter what happened here today, the scheme was over.

The moment FBI Agent John Graves was killed, the case could no longer be shoved under the rug by the locals.

"Put your weapons down, Rangers." Wes stepped from around the back of the railroad car, Sadie and Brandi beside him. "You're not arresting anyone."

Sadie cried out, "Let me go, Wes. You'll never have my son."

"Shut up, Sadie. I don't want the boy."

Sadie turned to Brandi. "He never did want a child. Said that a baby would ruin his life, until he laid eyes on him. A few months ago, Wes told his parents about Levi and now they want to take the child."

"That's enough, Sadie," the sheriff snapped.

Rhett stared at the man who'd taken him in and cared for him and Pam when they needed him most. "What's your part in this, Uncle?"

"Did you kill my dad?" Brandi asked, her voice strangely calm and even.

The sheriff glared at her. "We can come to a reasonable conclusion with all this."

Wes held a gun. "I told Sadie to stay away. Everything would've been all right if she had stayed away from Mulberry Gap. But no, you had to get all brave and contact the FBI before you came back. I had no choice but to let Coble know you were about to spill the beans." His cousin looked at Rhett. "She got into drugs. Sadie's a drughead."

"I don't think she was the only one, Wes." Rhett kept his eye on his uncle, wondering how much he knew and if he was involved in any of the crimes.

Wes moved toward the sheriff, taking the women with him.

"Far enough, son."

Wes turned on his father and asked, "Are you taking Rhett's side?"

"I can't do this anymore. Won't do this. I never should've protected you in the first place. I'd hoped you would come clean if you were given a chance. Drop your gun."

When Wes opened his mouth to talk, his dad pointed his gun and said, "Now."

Instead of dropping the weapon, he reared back and threw it across the junkyard.

Brandi looked at Rhett and Luke. "Coble used Wes and Sadie to steal the tornado fund, and then Wes killed Daddy. Coble blamed the sheriff and my dad for his son getting killed in prison, and thought the town owed him the tornado money. He wanted revenge."

"That's not true," Wes yelled. "It was an accident that Jordan got himself killed. Self-defense. It wasn't my fault."

The sheriff's shoulders sagged, and he shook his head. "It was Charlie's third offense. I had no choice."

The sheriff said to Rhett, "Read Wes and Dudley their rights."

Wes leaned forward. "I can't believe you're doing this, Dad. What kind of man arrests his own son? You've always preferred Rhett." As Luke went to put the handcuffs on the young man, Wes went into a screaming fit, trying to jerk away. But his dad helped subdue him as they slapped the handcuffs on and led him to the cruiser.

Rhett lowered his head and swallowed hard. He could only imagine the pain his uncle was feeling. Brandi had tried to tell him she hadn't trusted the sheriff's department, but Rhett hadn't wanted to believe it. Now he realized his uncle, the man he'd come to respect and love, had been involved in hurting the Callahans.

He glanced up at Brandi and his chest tightened. He was going to make this right. No matter how long it took, the lady he had once hoped to share his life with deserved his love and respect. If she could find it in her heart to give him the chance.

SEVENTEEN

Sadie sagged to the ground and Brandi ran to her side.

"What's wrong, sis?"

"I'm sick."

The frailness of her sister scared her. "What kind of sickness?"

"I'm sorry about Dad… It was all my fault. I never intended for any of this happen. We planned to pay back the money. Wes had gambling debts, and not just with the casinos, but he owed a couple of dangerous men who were threatening him. When Coble approached Wes about stealing the fund, Wes jumped at the opportunity. It seemed so easy. Coble promised to use his position with the sheriff's department to ward off any suspicions and to help point the investigation to Daddy and he'd pay Wes $100,000. Wes promised we'd pay the money back, or I never would've gone along with the scheme. It had sounded so harmless and easy. I accidentally found Dad's passwords to his computer a long time ago. Wes convinced me to access the bank computer remotely from home. I never dreamed Daddy would catch us, but he came home early from work. And then Wes killed him, and we took his body to the farm." Sadie's voice broke, and she covered her eyes with her hands. "It was awful. The sheriff helped him stage the suicide at the farm."

Brandi's heart sank. No wonder Sadie was afraid to come forward and had decided to disappear. The hurt was worse than any pain a bullet could produce. Instead of wanting to hide her sister's problems, Brandi just wanted to get help. For Sadie, for herself and Mom. Their family needed to pull together.

"What about Phil Sandford? Did he have anything to do with the money or Daddy's death?"

"Mr. Sandford? No, I don't think so."

Brandi sighed and put her arm around her sister and gently squeezed. "Let's go get Levi. I know he's ready to see you."

Tears clouded Sadie's eyes. "I have cancer."

"No." A lump formed in Brandi's throat. The statement couldn't have surprised her more. "Cancer? But how? You're so young."

Tears fell freely now. "Punishment for my sins."

"Oh no." Brandi tightened her hold on her younger sister. "That's not how God works. He's a forgiving God." As the words came out of her own mouth, she realized the hypocrisy of her attitude the last two years. She'd believed other families had their problems, but not hers. The pressure to be perfect was just too much.

No one was perfect.

As much as Brandi just wanted to hold her sister and take her home, she knew that couldn't happen yet. "The authorities will need to talk with you."

Rhett nodded and walked their way. "We have a lot to discuss."

Brandi's chest tightened. She knew Sadie would have

to reckon with the law. But she would be there for her sister.

After statements had been taken, Wes and the gunman were hauled off, and Rhett and Brandi brought Sadie to her mother's house. Rhett's aunt had contacted their mother two days ago to tell her the danger Brandi was in, and Mom and Phil were on their way home from the airport.

Brandi planned to stay with Sadie to make certain her sister was all right. Rhett said he wouldn't stay long, because they needed time alone. Pam was on her way with Levi. He strode to his truck to leave, and Brandi walked beside him.

The sky was clear, the stars out, and the night cool. She could've gone to her own home after Mom arrived, but Brandi didn't want to be alone tonight. Their family needed to be together to mend.

Rhett's silhouette stood out against the sparkly sky as he leaned against his truck. Chill bumps danced across her arms. A calm crossed over her. He'd never looked more handsome. Even though she wore a long-sleeved shirt, Rhett placed his heavy Western coat around her. She said, "I suppose you heard."

"About Sadie's cancer? I did. I'm sorry, Brandi."

"Why now?" Her shoulders slumped. "Am I going to lose her now that I found her?"

His arm went around her. "We're going to help her in every way we can. Through the treatments. With Levi…"

"With the criminal charges? Sadie's going to be charged, isn't she?"

"She probably won't get off totally, but it will go a long way that she contacted the FBI. Joe Dudley is the man who attacked you at the farm and shot Deputy Norris. Davin Ingram, the man subdued at the junkyard, was working off drug debts to Coble. The thirty-two-year-old was also at the airfield, but he had no desire to kill anyone. He's agreed to work with authorities. It'll take a while to sort through the evidence to find out who killed the agent. Dudley is blaming everything on Coble."

"Everything is such a mess." She rubbed her head. "What about Norris? Why did he pull his gun on me at the farm?"

"Still working on that one, but it looks like Norris may have been involved. He has a shiny new speedboat in his garage and a recent addition to his house. Ingram claims Norris was nervous about his involvement, and Coble was afraid he'd rat everyone out. Sounds like Coble was taking care of two birds with one stone when he sent Dudley to the farm."

Rhett glanced down at her, the intensity of his look sending a jolt through her. "I will stand beside you, Brandi, with whatever you need. We're in this together. You can trust me."

His words brought moisture to her eyes. In that moment, she knew his words were true.

His embrace tightened, the warmth penetrating through the coat. His breath tickled her neck. Oh, how she had missed him. Missed his touch. Missed his laugh. Missed the comfort he brought to her.

"I've changed." Rhett's mouth pressed against her ear, his voice deep. "You know, I tried to find Sadie when she disappeared, but I was also concerned about my job. Worried what the lieutenant would think. Looking back, I should've been up-front with him. Adcock would've understood."

She looked up into his stormy eyes dancing in the moonlight.

He said, "I'm sorry you felt I turned my back on you. I didn't mean to. My initial belief was that Sadie had struggled with your father's death and run away because she didn't know how to deal with it. But then the sheriff's department kept repeating foul play because she'd left her phone and her clothes. They believed she was dead or else she would've returned home. I should've known better."

Brandi swallowed, her mouth going dry. She'd waited to hear those words for so long, but now it didn't seem as important. For the first time in years, she was at peace. Not just with finding Sadie, but with her family, the town, Rhett—with herself.

"When you broke off our engagement, I was afraid to fight. Afraid what I would do if you kept going like my dad had. I should've taken the chance."

Her hand went to his chest, his heartbeat racing under her touch. "I should've been more patient."

"I've never stopped loving you." Without warning, he bent his head down and planted his lips against hers, bringing her to her toes. When he broke contact, the tingle from the kiss continued and her heart picked up pace.

"I want a future with you, Brandi." He shoved his hands into his pockets. "I want you back forever. Starting now."

"I want you, too." She smiled, her heart shaking a bit.

He pulled her into his arms and his lips pressed against hers again. "I love you."

In that moment, she knew she could finally put the past behind her, and the man she'd share her dreams with was standing in front of her. "I love you, too, Rhett Kincaid."

EPILOGUE

One year later

Brandi's heart warmed as she watched her husband set another tray of frosted cookies on the counter. Watching Rhett interact with the children from the homeless shelter brought her more joy than she believed possible. Not wanting to miss another minute of being together, she and Rhett had married last March.

A couple of young boys ran up and grabbed a handful of cookies before the platter settled on the counter. Christmas music played in the background and could barely be heard over the giggles and clamor of voices.

"What do you say?" Stormy asked the boys.

"Thank you," the kids said in unison.

"The children seem to be enjoying them." Estelle Callahan's face beamed. "Let me check on the turkey."

Her mom came into the kitchen with an empty tray. "I need another pitcher of punch."

"I'll get it." Sadie grabbed another half gallon of the red drink from the refrigerator and handed it to her mom.

It was good to see the family together again. Brandi had mended fences with her mom. Even Phil Sandford seemed to appreciate playing with Levi. The bank account in the Cayman Islands had been opened over four years ago when he and his first wife began to have marital problems. He'd kept the money from his wife so he wouldn't have to share it if they divorced. After the account became known, his ex-wife took him to court for her share of their money. Brandi had a difficult time comprehending how Mom found the man attractive, but she could see how much Mom missed Dad, and she understood Mom had looked to Phil for comfort.

Phil would never hold a candle to her dad, but maybe he made her mom feel loved. That was all Brandi wanted. Her family to be happy.

Grandma had sold the farm to her and Rhett at an affordable price for a wedding present, claiming she wanted the old home to be full of life and family again.

With Sadie and Levi staying with them, the home was overflowing with activity. Grandma visited at least once a month for Sunday dinner.

A year ago, Brandi wasn't certain her younger sister would live, but here Sadie was, celebrating Christmas with everyone. Sadie had completed her chemo treatments in the fall and would go back for her six-month checkup in March. If her health continued to improve, she planned to build a small home for her and Levi on the edge of the farm.

Sheriff Kincaid had lost his job and was serving a ten-year sentence for his part in the cover-up of her dad's death. His time would probably be cut in half for good behavior. She was saddened to see Rhett's uncle in jail, but the sheriff's lawyer was working on an appeal. Wes received twenty years. Aunt Lauren had moved to New York to live near her daughter. Brandi wondered if the woman would stick by her husband's side or finally move on with her life.

Rhett took Brandi's hands into his. "This is the best Christmas I can remember."

"Me, too." The feeling of belonging overwhelmed her. "What could be better than being surrounded by family?"

He grinned. "Spending time alone with you isn't so bad, you know."

Her choice of words dawned on her. "Oh, I'm sorry. I didn't mean anything about your family."

"I know what you meant." His shrugged. "My uncle had to pay for his crimes, though, and he understood that. I wished he had talked with me, but that wasn't his style."

Duke Kincaid had been the source of heartbreak for Rhett. What the man gave up trying to help his son, albeit unlawful, was monumental. Rhett visited him often in prison. The chance of Wes changing was unlikely, but with prayer and love, a person could overcome anything.

Stormy stepped into the room. "The kids are ready to open their presents."

Rhett and Brandi pulled apart.

The woman moved closer. "This is the best Christmas most of these kids have ever seen. I can't tell you how much I appreciate all you've done for the shelter over the past year."

Rhett looked down at her. "You're the one who keeps things running smoothly."

Stormy shook her head, not ever seeming to take the compliments. "Let's not keep the children waiting."

Brandi started to follow Stormy, but then a strange fluttering brought her to a halt.

"What is it?"

"Come here." She smiled as she took Rhett's hand and

placed it on her belly. There it was again. A tiny flickering. "Did you feel that?"

His lips lifted at the corners into a smile. "Is that the baby?"

"Yes." She nodded, a smile spreading across her face. "I'm only seventeen weeks along, so I didn't think it would happen for another few weeks. I can't wait for little Jordan to get here."

"Your dad would be proud. You know that, right?"

She nodded. "Yeah, I do. Sometimes I expect him to walk through the door and join us. I miss him every day, but after Sadie returned home, I feel as though we've healed."

Rhett pulled her close and she laid her head on his shoulder as they walked into the living room. Kids of all ages sat on the furniture and on the floor, waiting to open their gifts.

He leaned over and whispered, "You're the best present a guy could ever wish for. I love you, Brandi Kincaid."

"I love you, too."

* * * * *

If you liked this story from Connie Queen,
check out her previous
Love Inspired Suspense book:

Justice Undercover

Available now from Love Inspired Suspense!

Find more great reads at www.LoveInspired.com.

Dear Reader,

I'm excited to share Rhett and Brandi's story with you. Brandi has been dealing with trust issues since her father was accused of theft and the image of her perfect family came tumbling down. She believes her lifelong friends turned their back on her, and now she aims to prove them wrong and restore her family's reputation. Abandoned as a child, Rhett also struggles to believe in others, so when Brandi breaks off their wedding engagement, he's afraid to fight to win her back.

Have you ever been in a situation where your confidence takes a blow, and you feel alone? What did you do to make things better? Did you lean on God or try to handle it yourself? I hope you can relate to Rhett and Brandi and overcome as they do.

Connie Queen

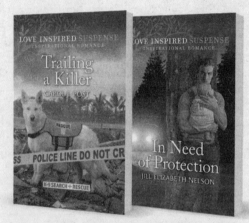

COMING NEXT MONTH FROM
Love Inspired Suspense

BLIZZARD SHOWDOWN
Alaska K-9 Unit • by Shirlee McCoy
After months of searching for Violet James, Gabriel Runyon and his K-9 partner finally track her down—just in time to rescue her from her ex-fiancé. Now it's up to them to safeguard the single mother and her newborn daughter. But can they outrun a blizzard *and* an enemy who wants Violet dead?

CHRISTMAS K-9 PROTECTORS
Alaska K-9 Unit • by Lenora Worth and Maggie K. Black
Members of the K-9 team face danger and find love in these holiday novellas, in which a rookie K-9 trooper and his furry partner must save a forensic scientist from a ruthless jewelry thief, and a tech whiz, a criminal psychologist and a K-9 go on the run to keep a teen out of the hands of a kidnapping gang.

AMISH CHRISTMAS ESCAPE
Amish Country Justice • by Dana R. Lynn
In the sights of a murderer, Christy O'Malley knows there is just one person she can rely on to shield her—her estranged husband, who doesn't know he is a father. But when she shows up on Sam Burkholder's doorstep in Amish country, can he help her and their little girl live through Christmas?

CHRISTMAS VENDETTA
Emergency Responders • by Valerie Hansen
Teacher Sandy Lynn Forrester's peaceful Christmas vacation is interrupted when somebody tries to kill her—but the cops don't think the threat is real. The only person who believes her is a man she doesn't trust: framed and discredited cop Clay Danforth. But with her life on the line, he's her best chance at survival...

CAPTURED AT CHRISTMAS
by Jodie Bailey
Undercover with an infantry unit to investigate the theft of hard drives, military investigator Captain Rachel Blake doesn't expect the holiday assignment to turn into a protection mission. But when Captain Marshall Slater and his little girl are targeted, she'll risk everything to help keep them safe.

WYOMING CHRISTMAS PERIL
by Kathie Ridings
Fleeing from a murderous bank robber at Christmastime, Bailey O'Keefe has only FBI agent Sean Hanson to protect her. But when their safe house is breached, can Bailey and Sean outmaneuver their enemy while battling the elements and the hazards of the snow-packed trails on Cougar Mountain?

LOOK FOR THESE AND OTHER LOVE INSPIRED BOOKS WHEREVER BOOKS ARE SOLD, INCLUDING MOST BOOKSTORES, SUPERMARKETS, DISCOUNT STORES AND DRUGSTORES.

LISCNM1121

Sounds of a scuffle woke Clay Danforth. He stared up at
the ceiling and saw the light fixture vibrate. Whatever
was happening on the floor above him was violent, which
did not bode well for the residents of that apartment.

He listened carefully, seeking confirmation of his
initial conclusion. It came in the form of a woman's
scream. It didn't matter that he hadn't yet met his
neighbors. Somebody up there needed him, and although
his authority had ended when he'd left the police force,
his concern for fellow citizens had not. He pulled on
jeans and boots, palmed his phone long enough to call
911, then slipped a gun into the waistband at the small of
his back and headed for the stairway.

Taking the steps two at a time, he rounded the corner
and saw a partially open door. Raised voices identified
that apartment as the source of the conflict. A woman's
screeching demand to be left alone spurred him into a
run.

Slamming his shoulder against the outer wall next to the doorjamb, he drew the gun. "Police! Come out with your hands up."

In moments a black-clad figure raced past him and pounded down the stairs. Without knowing any details, Clay didn't dare shoot; nor was it prudent to give chase.

Anticipating a second criminal or more, Clay whipped around the corner and took a shooter's stance in the doorway. Something whizzed past his ear and clipped the edge of his shoulder. "Stop! I'm a police officer." Which was sort of still true.

He diverted his aim. His free hand shot out to grab the metal shaft of the club. When he focused on the person holding the leather grip, the effect was mind-blowing. Looking into those familiar hazel eyes, he croaked, "Sandy?"

The impossibility that he would have chosen an apartment directly beneath Sandy Lynn Forrester, the one woman who had shattered his heart into a thousand pieces, was not only astounding, but it made him furious with the friend who had talked him into the lease. He would never have listened to Abe and signed the contract if he'd dreamed she lived in the same building. Never in a million years.